# THE WINTER MURDER CASE

# THE WINTER MURDER CASE

S. S. Van Dine

FELONY & MAYHEM PRESS • NEW YORK

*All the characters and events portrayed in this work are fictitious.*

THE WINTER MURDER CASE

A Felony & Mayhem mystery

PRINTING HISTORY
First edition (Scribner's): 1939

Felony & Mayhem edition: 2021

Copyright © 1939 by Charles Scribner's Sons
Copyright renewed 1954 by Claire R. Wright

All rights reserved

ISBN: 978-1-63194-207-5

Manufactured in the United States of America

Cataloging-in-Publication information for this book
is available from the Library of Congress

Stern Winter loves a dirge-like sound.
—*Wordsworth*

# CONTENTS

# CHARACTERS OF THE BOOK

| | |
|---|---|
| PHILO VANCE | |
| JOHN F.-X. MARKHAM | *District Attorney of New York County* |
| ELLA GUNTHAR | *Companion to Joan Rexon* |
| CARRINGTON REXON | *Owner of the Rexon estate* |
| RICHARD REXON | *His son* |
| JOAN REXON | *His invalid daughter* |
| CARLOTTA NAESMITH | *Prominent society girl* |
| DOCTOR LOOMIS QUAYNE | *The Rexon family physician* |
| JACQUES BASSETT | *A friend of Richard Rexon* |
| ERIC GUNTHAR | *Father of Ella Gunthar Overseer on the Rexon estate* |
| MARCIA BRUCE | *The Rexon housekeeper* |
| OLD JED | *The Green Hermit Former overseer on the Rexon estate* |
| LIEUTENANT O'LEARY | *Lieutenant of the Winewood police* |
| LIEF WALLEN | *A guard on the Rexon estate* |
| GUY DARRUP | *Chief carpenter on the Rexon estate* |

| | |
|---|---|
| JOHN BRANDER | *Coroner* |
| HIGGINS | *The Rexon butler* |
| DAHLIA DUNHAM | *Political aspirant*<br>*Guest at the Rexon estate* |
| SALLY ALEXANDER | *Singer and impersonator*<br>*Guest at the Rexon estate* |
| BEATRICE MADDOX | *Famous aviatrix*<br>*Guest at the Rexon estate* |
| STANLEY SYDES | *Treasure hunter*<br>*Guest at the Rexon estate* |
| PAT MCORSAY | *Racing driver*<br>*Guest at the Rexon estate* |
| CHUCK THROME | *Gentleman jockey*<br>*Guest at the Rexon estate* |

The icon above says you're holding a copy of a book in the Felony & Mayhem "Vintage" category. These books were originally published prior to about 1965, and feature the kind of twisty, ingenious puzzles beloved by fans of Agatha Christie and John Dickson Carr. If you enjoy this book, you may well like other "Vintage" titles from Felony & Mayhem Press.

ANTHONY BERKELEY

*The Poisoned Chocolates Case*

ELIZABETH DALY

*Unexpected Night*
*Deadly Nightshade*
*Murders in Volume 2*
*The House without the Door*
*Evidence of Things Seen*
*Nothing Can Rescue Me*
*Arrow Pointing Nowhere*
*The Book of the Dead*
*Any Shape or Form*
*Somewhere in the House*
*The Wrong Way Down*
*Night Walk*
*The Book of the Lion*
*And Dangerous to Know*
*Death and Letters*
*The Book of the Crime*

NGAIO MARSH

*A Man Lay Dead*
*Enter a Murderer*
*The Nursing Home Murder*
*Death in Ecstasy*
*Vintage Murder*
*Artists in Crime*
*Death in a White Tie*
*Overture to Death*
*Death at the Bar*
*Surfeit of Lampreys*
*Death and the Dancing Footman*
*Colour Scheme*
*Died in the Wool*
*Final Curtain*
*Swing, Brother, Swing*
*Night at the Vulcan*
*Spinsters in Jeopardy*
*Scales of Justice*
*Death of a Fool*
*Singing in the Shrouds*
*False Scent*
*Hand in Glove*

NGAIO MARSH (*cont.*)
*Dead Water*
*Killer Dolphin*
*Clutch of Constables*
*When in Rome*
*Tied Up in Tinsel*
*Black as He's Painted*
*Last Ditch*
*A Grave Mistake*
*Photo Finish*
*Light Thickens*
*Collected Short Mysteries*

PATRCIA MOYES
*Dead Men Don't Ski*
*The Sunken Sailor*
*Death on the Agenda*
*Murder à la Mode*
*Falling Star*
*Johnny Under Ground*
*Murder Fantastical*
*Death and the Dutch Uncle*
*Who Saw Her Die?*
*Season of Snow and Sins*
*The Curious Affair of the Third Dog*
*Black Widower*

PATRCIA MOYES (*cont.*)
*The Coconut Killings*
*Who Is Simon Warwick?*
*Angel Death*
*A Six-Letter Word for Death*
*Night Ferry to Death*
*Black Girl, White Girl*

LENORE GLEN OFFORD
*Skeleton Key*
*The Glass Mask*
*The Smiling Tiger*
*My True Love Lies*
*The 9 Dark Hours*

S.S. VAN DINE
*The Benson Murder Case*
*The Canary Murder Case*
*The Greene Murder Case*
*The Bishop Murder Case*
*The Scarab Murder Case*
*The Kennel Murder Case*
*The Dragon Murder Case*
*The Casino Murder Case*
*The Garden Murder Case*
*The Kidnap Murder Case*
*The Gracie Allen Murder Case*

For more about these books, and other Felony & Mayhem titles, or to place an order, please visit our website at:

www.FelonyAndMayhem.com

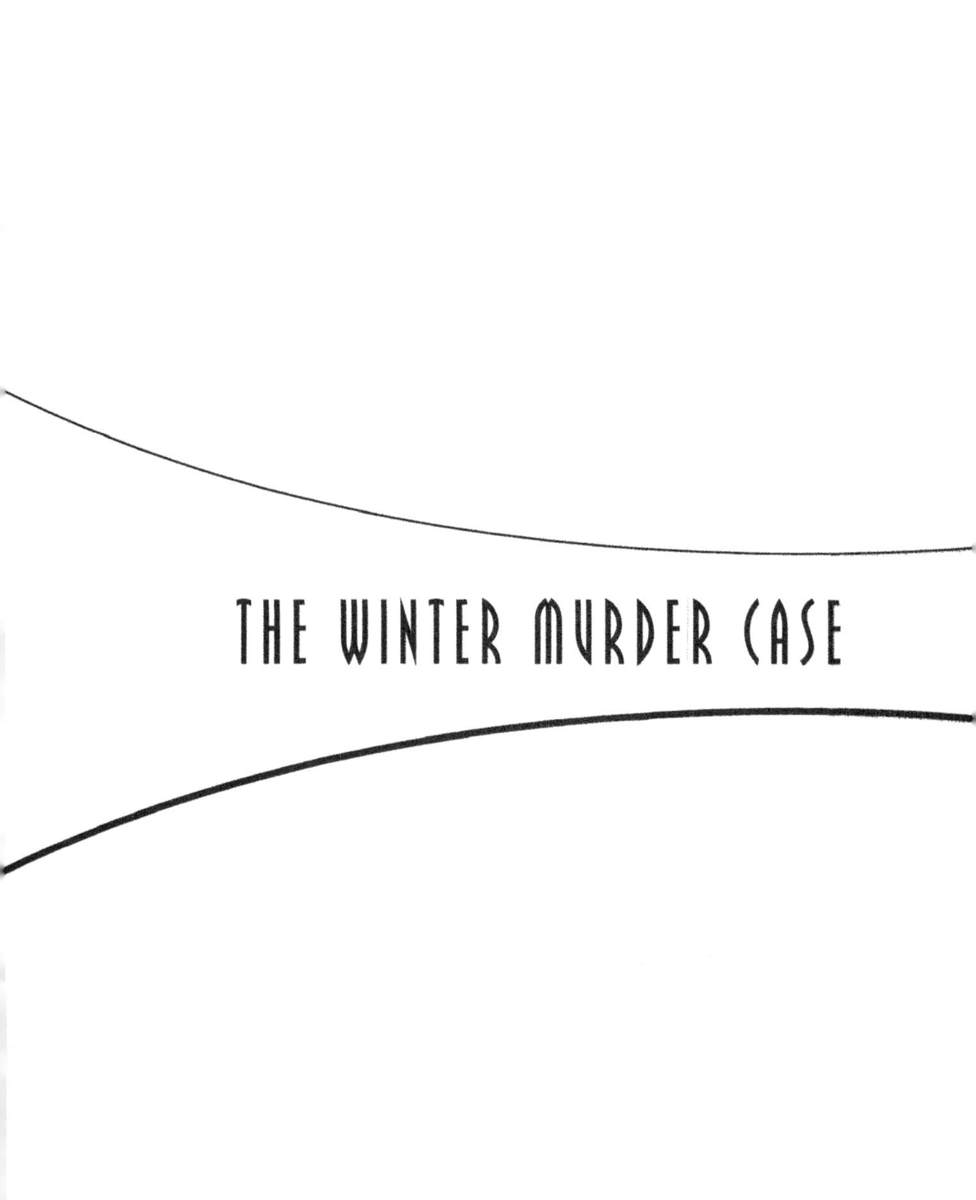
THE WINTER MURDER CASE

# PREFACE

IT WAS CHARACTERISTIC of Willard Huntington Wright, known to the great public as S. S. Van Dine, that when he died suddenly on April 11, 1939, he left *The Winter Murder Case* in the form in which it is published, complete to the last comma. Everything he ever did was done that way, accurately, thoroughly, and with consideration for other people. It was so with the entire series of the Philo Vance mysteries.

He has himself told the story of becoming a writer of mysteries in an article called, "I Used to be a Highbrow, and Look at Me Now." He had worked as a critic of literature and art, and as an editor, since he left Harvard in 1907. And this he had done with great distinction, but with no material reward to speak of—certainly no accumulation of money. When the war came it seemed to him that all he had believed in and was working for was rushing into ruin—and now, twenty-five years later, can anyone say he was wrong? There were other influences at work on him perhaps, but no one who knew

Willard and the purity of his perceptions in art, and his devotion to what he thought was the meaning of our civilization as expressed in the arts, can doubt that the shattering disillusionment and ruin of the war was what brought him at last to a nervous breakdown which incapacitated him for several years. He would never have explained it so, or any other way. He made no explanations, or excuses, ever, and his many apologies were out of the kindness of a heart so concealed by reticence that only a handful ever knew how gentle it really was. So at last all that he had done and aimed to do seemed to have come to ruin, and he himself too.

Only a gallant spirit could have risen up from that downfall, and gallantry alone would not have been enough. But Willard had also an intellect—even despair could not suppress it—which worked on anything at hand. One might believe that if his fate had been solitary confinement he would have emerged with some biological discovery based on the rats that infested his cell. Anyhow, his doctor finally met his demands for mental occupation with the concession that he read mysteries, which he had never read before. The result was, that as he had studied painting, literature and philosophy, he now involuntarily studied and then consciously analyzed the mystery story. And when he recovered he had mastered it.

He was then heavily in debt, but he thought he saw the possibility of freeing himself from obligations a nature of his integrity could not ignore, or in fact endure, by what he had learned in his illness. He wrote out, at some ten thousand words each, the plots of his first three murder cases, thought through to the last detail, footnotes and all, and brought them to the Century Club to a lunch with an editor of the publishing house that has put all of them before the public.

This editor knew little about mystery stories, which had not been much in vogue since Sherlock Holmes, but he knew Willard Wright. He knew from far back in Harvard that whatever this man did would be done well, and the reasonable terms—granting the writer's talent—that Willard proposed were quickly accepted.

It is now thirteen years since Philo Vance stepped out into the world to solve *The Benson Murder Case* and, with that and the eleven others that followed, to delight hundreds of thousands of readers soon hard pressed by the anxieties and afflictions of a tragic decade. Each of these famous cases was set forth, as were the first three, in a long synopsis—about ten thousand words—letter perfect and complete to that point in its development. After the first three of these synopses, the publisher never saw another, nor wanted to, for he knew beyond peradventure that the finished book would be another masterpiece in its kind. Nor did he ever see the second stage of development, but only the third, the final manuscript—and that he read with the interest and pleasure of any reader, and with no professional anxieties. But this second stage in the infinitely painstaking development of the story was some 30,000 words long, and it lacked only the final elaboration of character, dialogue, and atmosphere. *The Winter Murder Case* represents this stage in S. S. Van Dine's progress to its completion, and if the plot moves faster to its culmination than in the earlier books, it is for that reason.

They say now that Philo Vance was made in the image of S. S. Van Dine, and although Willard smoked not *Régies* but denicotined cigarettes, there were resemblances. Both were infinitely neat in dress, equally decorous and considerate in manner, and Vance had Willard's amazingly vast and accurate knowledge of a thousand arts and subjects, and his humorously sceptical attitude toward life and society. But in fact the resemblance would stand for only those with a superficial knowledge of Willard Huntington Wright. Vance in so far as he was Wright, was perhaps the form under which a gallant, gentle man concealed a spirit almost too delicate and sensitive for an age so turbulent and crude as this. Willard was not one to wear his heart upon his sleeve—but there were daws enough to peck, as there always are, and they found it where his friends always knew it to be, near the surface, and quick to respond.

As for the principles upon which he based his writing, and which brought new life into the craft of detective literature, they were succinctly set down by him in his famous twenty rules which are to be found at the back of this volume.

# CHAPTER ONE

## *An Appeal for Help*

*(Tuesday, January 14; 11 a.m.)*

"HOW WOULD YOU like a brief vacation in ideal surroundings—winter sports, pleasing company, and a veritable mansion in which to relax? I have just such an invitation for you, Vance."

Philo Vance drew on his cigarette and smiled. We had just arrived at District Attorney Markham's office in answer to a facetious yet urgent call. Vance looked at him and sighed.

"I suspect you. Speak freely, my dear Rhadamanthus."

"Old Carrington Rexon's worried."

"Ah!" Vance drawled. "No spontaneous goodness of heart in life. Sad. So, I'm asked to enjoy myself in the Berkshires only because Carrington Rexon's worried. A detective on the premises would soothe his harassed spirits. I'm invited. Not flatterin'. No."

"Don't be cynical, Vance."

"But why should Carrington Rexon's worries concern me? *I*'m not in the least worried."

"You will be," said Markham with feigned viciousness. "Don't deny you dote on the sufferings of others, you sadist.

You live for crime and suffering. And you adore worrying. You'd die of ennui if all were peaceful."

"Tut, tut," returned Vance. "Not sadistic. No. Always strivin' for peace and calm. My charitable, unselfish nature."

"As I thought! Old Rexon's worry *does* appeal to you. I detect the glint in your eye."

"Charming place, the Rexon estate," Vance observed thoughtfully. "But why, Markham, with his millions, his leisure, his two adored and adoring offspring, his gorgeous estate, his fame, and his vigor—why should he be worrying? Quite unreasonable."

"Still, he wants you up there instanter."

"As you said." Vance settled deeper into his chair. "His emeralds, I opine, are to blame for his qualms."

Markham looked across at the other shrewdly.

"Don't be clairvoyant. I detest soothsayers. Especially when their guesses are so obvious. Of course, it's his damned emeralds."

"Tell me all. Leave no precious stone unturned. Could you bear it?"

Markham lighted a cigar. When he had it going he said:

"No need to tell you of Rexon's famous emerald collection. You probably know how it's safeguarded."

"Yes," said Vance. "I inspected it some years ago. Inadequately protected, I thought."

"The same today. Thank Heaven the place isn't in my jurisdiction: I'd be worrying about it constantly. I once tried to persuade Rexon to transfer the collection to some museum."

"Not nice of you, Markham. Rexon loves his gewgaws fanatically. He'd wither away if bereft of his emeralds... Oh, why are collectors?"

"I'm sure I don't know. I didn't make the world."

"Regrettable," sighed Vance. "What is toward?"

"An unpredictable situation at the Rexon estate. The old boy's apprehensive. Hence his desire for your presence."

"More light, please."

"Rexon Manor," continued Markham, "is at present filled with guests as a result of young Richard Rexon's furlough: the chap has just returned from Europe where he has been studying medicine intensively in the last-word European colleges and hospitals. The old man's giving a kind of celebration in the boy's honor—"

"I know. And hoping for an announcement of Richard's betrothal to the blue-blooded Carlotta Naesmith. Still, why his anxiety?"

"Rexon being a widower, with an invalid daughter, asked Miss Naesmith to arrange a house party and celebration. She did—with a vengeance. Mostly café society: weird birds, quite objectionable to old Rexon's staid tastes. He doesn't understand this new set; is inclined to distrust them. He doesn't suspect them, exactly, but their proximity to his precious emeralds gives him the jitters."

"Old-fashioned chap. The new generation *is* full of incredible possibilities. Not a lovable and comfortable lot. Does Rexon point specifically?"

"Only at a fellow named Bassett. And, strangely enough, he's not of Miss Naesmith's doing. Acquaintance of Richard's, in fact. Friendship started abroad—in Switzerland, I believe. Came over on the boat with him this last trip. But the old gentleman admits he has no grounds for his uneasiness. He's just nervous, in a vague way, about the whole situation. Wants perspicacious companionship. So he phoned me and asked for help, indicating you."

"Yes. Collectors are like that. Where can he turn in his hour of uncertainty? Ah, his old friend Markham! Equipped with all the proper gadgets for just such delicate observation. Gadget Number One: Mr. Philo Vance. Looks presentable in a dinner coat. Won't drink from his finger-bowl. Could mingle and observe, without rousing suspicion. Discretion guaranteed. Excellent way of detecting a lurking shadow—if any." Vance smiled resignedly. "Is that the gist of the worried Rexon's runes by long-distance phone?"

"Substantially, yes," admitted Markham. "But expressed more charitably. You know damned well that old Rexon likes you, and that if he thought you'd care for the house party, you'd have been more than welcome."

"You shame me, Markham," Vance returned with contrition. "I'm fond of Rexon, just as you are. A lovable man… So, he craves my comfortin' presence. Very well, I shall strive to smooth his furrowed brow."

# CHAPTER TWO

## *Glamor in the Moonlight*

*(Wednesday, January 15; 9 p.m.)*

MARKHAM NOTIFIED CARRINGTON Rexon, and we left New York the following afternoon in Vance's Hispano-Suiza.

It was a cold, clear day, and fresh snow had fallen during the night. The drive to Winewood in the Berkshires would ordinarily have taken about five hours, but the roads north of the city were deep in snow, and we were late in arriving at the Rexon estate. Darkness had settled early, but the night was white with stars, and the moon was luminous.

It was nearly nine o'clock when we turned in through a wide stone gateway that marked the outer limits of the vast estate. There was no one to direct us, and when we had reached the crest of a high rocky hill, Vance was confused as to which turning to take. There were half-hidden tracks in one of the forks of the narrow road, and we turned to the right to follow them.

A mile or so farther on, the road sloped gently downward into a narrow snowclad valley at the far end of which precipitous cliffs rose to a tree-crested plateau. Vance let the car coast noiselessly into the still white fairyland.

As we reached the base of the long incline the sound of faint music came to us through the trees on our left. There was no habitation visible, and the music intensified the fantasy of the setting which spread before us.

Applying the brakes, Vance stopped the car and, stepping out, moved towards the source of the lilting notes.

We had gone scarcely a hundred yards when, through the trees which hid us from view, we spied a small frozen pond on which a girl was skating. The music came from a small portable phonograph placed on a rustic bench at the edge of the pond.

The girl, in a simple white skating costume, seemed unreal in the light of the moon and stars. She was going through one difficult skating figure after another with serious repetition, as if trying to perfect their intricacies. Vance suddenly became attentive.

"My word!" he whispered. "Magnificent skating!"

He stood fascinated by the girl's proficiency as she executed various school figures and complicated free routines.

The phonograph ran down and, as the girl completed an involved jump and spiral spin, Vance approached her with a cheerful greeting. At first she was startled; then she smiled shyly.

"You must be new guests at the Manor," she remarked in a timid voice. "I'm so sorry you caught me skating. It's sort of a secret, you see… Maybe you won't tell anyone," she added with a note of appeal in her voice.

"Of course, we shan't." Vance studied the girl critically. "I believe I remember you—I was at the Manor some years ago. Weren't you the friend and companion of Miss Joan?"

She nodded. "I was. And I still am. I'm Ella Gunthar. But I don't remember you. It must have been when I was a little girl."

"My name is Philo Vance," Vance told her. "I was just driving to the Manor, and lost my way. When I heard your music I came over in the hope of finding my bearings."

"You're not seriously lost," she said. "This is the Green Glen and if you go back up the hill and take the narrow road to the right for about a mile, you'll see the Manor just ahead."

Vance thanked her, but lingered a moment. "Tell me, Miss Gunthar: if you are Joan's companion at the Manor, why do you skate on this little pond so far away from the main house?"

The girl's lovely face seemed to cloud for a moment.

"I—I don't want to hurt Joan's feelings," she answered cryptically. "I always come to the Green Glen at night when my duties are over at the Manor, to do my skating."

"But the phonograph," said Vance; "isn't it frightfully heavy to carry all this way?"

"Oh, I don't keep it at the Manor." She laughed. "I keep it in Jed's hut, just around the curve in the road, by that big cypress tree. And I keep my skates and skating clothes there, too. It's all a secret between Jed and me."

Vance smiled at her reassuringly.

"Well, I promise the secret will go no farther. But it's really a magnificent secret. You know, don't you, that you skate beautifully? You're one of the most talented performers I have ever seen."

The girl blushed with pleasure.

"I love skating," she replied simply.

A few minutes later we had turned into the driveway to the brilliantly lighted Rexon Manor.

As a bald elderly butler led us through the lower hall we could hear the boisterous hilarity of many guests in the drawing room—snatches of popular music, laughter, raised voices: a gay and youthful clamor.

Carrington Rexon, alone in his den, greeted us with old-world dignity. It was the first time I had met him, but I was not unfamiliar with his features, as pictures of him had frequently appeared in the Metropolitan press. He was a tall, slender, impressive man in his sixties; aloof and stern, and with an imperious air of feudalism. He vaguely suggested Sargent's famous portrait of Lord Ribblesdale.

"Ah, Vance! It was generous of you to come. Perhaps you think I am unduly apprehensive..."

The door opened and a dark, serious young man of athletic build stood on the threshold.

Rexon turned without surprise.

"My son Richard," he informed us with undisguised pride. Then: "But why are you deserting our guests?"

"I'm a bit fed up." Then the young man shrugged his shoulders apologetically and smiled. "I guess I'm not used to it. It's such a change—"

A girl of about twenty-five appeared in the doorway and looked about.

The elder Rexon somewhat relaxed his stern manner and presented us. Her likeness, too, I had seen many times in the New York papers. Carlotta Naesmith had been a vivid and gifted debutante a few years before. She was a colorful auburn-haired young woman, animated and vital, with sagacious eyes and an air of self-assurance. She nodded to us casually, and turned to young Rexon.

"Completely overcome, Dick? Has the gaiety got you down? Come, don't desert the ship just when the sea's getting stormy."

"I think Carlotta is quite right, Richard," Carrington Rexon commented. "You came home for relaxation. Forget your scalpels and microbes for a while. Go on back with Carlotta, and take Mr. Vance with you. He'll want to meet your friends."

# CHAPTER THREE

## *The Bourbon Glass*

*(Wednesday, January 15; 10:30 p.m.)*

AN UNUSUALLY GAY and colorful sight confronted us in the great drawing room. Groups of young people stood about joking and laughing; others danced. A spirit of carefree revelry animated the scene.

Carlotta Naesmith was a capable hostess. She led us through the boisterous throng, introducing us haphazardly.

"This is Dahlia Dunham," she said, snaring a wiry and tense young woman of perhaps thirty. "Dahlia's a political spellbinder, full of incredible phrases, and death to hecklers. She'll stump for any cause from Socialism to Fletcherism—"

"But not for prohibition, dear," the other retorted in a raucous unsteady voice, as she withdrew her arm from Miss Naesmith's and hurried toward the miniature bar.

Another girl came up, complaining.

"A hell of a place! No landing field! When you snare the Rexon millions, Carlotta, see to it that Dick builds one."

She was blonde and frail, with liquid eyes that dominated her pointed face. I recognized the much publicized Beatrice

Maddox before Carlotta Naesmith presented us. She had recently won fame as an airplane pilot, and only a governmental veto had stayed her proposed solo flight across the Atlantic.

"What's up, Bee?" came a rumbling voice behind me, and a young Irish giant threw his arms about Miss Maddox. "You look glum. Out of gas? So am I." He whisked her away to the bar.

"That was Pat McOrsay," Miss Naesmith told us. "He drives 'em fast. Won last year's auto grind at Cincinnati. He's sweet on Bee, but she holds mere auto racers in contempt. Maybe they'll compromise. I did want you to meet Pat—he's such a beast... But wait. There's another speed demon of a kind over there... Hi there, Chuck," she called across the room. "Stop trying to tout Sally and come over here a moment—if you can make it."

Chuck Throme, the internationally famous gentleman jockey who had won the last Steeplechase at Aintree, staggered stiffly up. His eyes wouldn't focus, but his manner was impeccable.

"Sit down, darling, and meet Mr. Vance," Miss Naesmith exhorted. "Don't try it standing up. Your stirrups'll bend."

Throme drew himself up indignantly to his five-feet-five and bowed with a Chestertonian flourish. But the supreme gesture was not completed. He continued his obeisance to the rug and lay there.

"That's one race Chuck didn't win," laughed our *cicerone*. "Let's move on. Some assistant starter will put him back in the saddle... Isn't it positively disgusting, Mr. Vance? Liquor is a frightful curse. Saps the brain, undermines the morals, and all that... Which reminds me: let's take an intermission in our round of social duties and have a drink."

She led us to the bar.

"I'm very demure—for Richard's sake. I drink only Dubonnet in public. But don't let my girlish restraint affect your batting average. Everything's available, including trinitrotoluene."

Vance drank brandy. As we stood chatting a tall, rugged, sunburnt man came up and put his arms possessively about Miss Naesmith.

"I'm still yearning to know your answer, Carlotta," he blustered good-naturedly. "For the next-to-the-last time: Are you, or are you not, coming with me to Cocos Island when Dick returns to his bone-sawing?"

"Ha!" Carlotta Naesmith swung about and pushed him away playfully. "Still crooning your Once-Aboard-the-Lugger ditty. You're inelegant, Stan. And right under Dick's nose."

Richard Rexon showed no annoyance. He came forward and, putting one hand on the other man's arm, introduced him to us. It was Stanley Sydes, a young society man with too much money, who spent his time on expeditions in quest of buried treasure.

Vance knew of his exploits, and a brief discussion took place.

"A playboy bulging with good money who spends it hunting dirty doubloons!" Carlotta Naesmith laughed. "There's a paradox—or is the whole world crazy except me?"

"Not a paradox, Miss Naesmith," Vance put in pleasantly. "I understand Mr. Sydes' urge perfectly. It's really not the treasure, y' know. It's the quest."

"Right!" boomed Sydes. "The joy of outwitting others, of solving riddles; and the acquisition of the unique... Hell, I'm talking like a collector—Forgive me, Richard. No offense to your eminent sire." A noisy group opposite attracted his attention, and he joined them.

His place at the bar was taken almost immediately by the girl who had been bantering with Throme.

"My God, Sally!" Miss Naesmith greeted her. "Really alone? Hasn't your gentleman jockey regained his mount?... Gentlemen,"—she turned to us—"we have here none other than Sally Alexander, the inimitable—pride of the Purple Room, off-color raconteuse and pianist extraordinary. A one-woman slum. She carried the Blue Book to the masses—and made 'em like it. A feat, egad!"

"I'm being maligned, gents," Sally Alexander protested. "I'm elegant, no end."

"I quite agree," Vance defended her. "I've heard Miss Alexander sing, and never once have I blushed."

"That must have been when she sang in the village choir, in her sub-deb days."

"Just for that," retorted Miss Alexander, "I'm going to take Dick away from you." And, slipping her arm through Richard Rexon's, she led him to the dance floor.

Miss Naesmith shrugged. She looked at Vance.

"Had enough of this, Sir Galahad? There are other exhibits in the zoo. Nothing really special, however. Am I not an honest guide?"

"Honest and charming." Vance set down his glass. "But isn't there a Mr. Bassett?"

"Oh, Jacques..." She looked round the room. "He's Richard's friend, you know. A more or less imported specimen, I believe. Anyway, he came over on the boat with Dick and is always comparing our ski runs with those of Switzerland—to the detriment of ours, of course. Maybe he does yodel and live on goat's milk. I wouldn't know. Though I do know he speaks American with a prairie accent—if my ears don't lie."

She caught sight of Bassett.

"There's your man, in the far corner, drinking lustily by himself. Come along. You can have him gladly. Then I'll go and rescue Dick. Sally'll be at the risqué-story stage by now."

Jacques Bassett sat at a small table, drinking Bourbon. He was tall, dark, aggressively athletic. His heavy eyebrows met over a broad flat nose.

He talked about Europe. Vance showed interest. Swiss winter resorts came up. Vance asked questions. Bassett expatiated. He was eloquent about the toboggan runs and the ski trails at Oberlachen in the Tyrol. Vance mentioned Amsterdam. But the subject had no interest for Bassett. He wandered away.

Vance turned his back. Then he threw his handkerchief over the glass from which Bassett had been drinking. Slipping it into his pocket, he left the room abruptly.

A little later, I found Vance with Carrington Rexon in the den. Another man was seated with them before the log fire. He was in his late forties, with steel-grey hair, and a soft voice which seemed to cover a tension: obviously a man of the world, with a highly professional manner which was rigid, but not without ingratiation. I was not surprised to find that he was Doctor Loomis Quayne, the Rexon physician.

"Doctor Quayne," Rexon explained, "dropped by to see my daughter Joan. But the excitement of so many guests has wearied her and she retired long ago." His voice was wistful.

(Vance had told me during our drive to Winewood something of Joan Rexon's tragedy: how she had fallen and injured her spine while skating, when she was only ten years old.)

"Joan's fatigue need not worry you, my dear Rexon," the doctor assured him. "It's natural in the circumstances. This little excitement may do her good, in fact—stimulate her interest, lead her mind along new lines. Psychological therapy is our chief recourse just now… I'll drop in again tomorrow. I hope I'll see Richard then, too. I've hardly talked with him since he came. But I'm glad to find him looking as well as when I saw him on my trip abroad two years ago."

"Dick's in the drawing room now," Rexon suggested with a twinkle.

The doctor smiled. "No, not this evening. I must be going soon. I left the motor of my car running so I won't have to bother priming it. These cold days the starter doesn't work so well… And I think I prefer the quiet of your den, if I may sit and finish my highball."

"Can't say that I blame you, doctor… This new generation…" Rexon shook his head disapprovingly.

As we talked on, largely in generalities, but with an occasional allusion to Richard Rexon's future in medicine, it became evident that there was something deeper than the mere professional relationship between Rexon and Quayne; a touch of intimacy, perhaps, due to long and tragic association.

At length the doctor rose and bade us good night. Vance and I left Carrington Rexon shortly after.

"A strange and dizzy household." Vance sprawled in an easy chair in his room. "No wonder old Rexon's jittery. Probably feels lost in the midst of the unknown. Obviously determined on Carlotta as a daughter-in-law, though; he's just the type to crave a dynastic marriage for his son. And the girl's not deficient in gifts. Nice; but too vivid for my aging tastes. And Richard. An admirable chap. Too serious for this outfit. Strange, too, his attitude toward Carlotta. Not all it should be. Seemed quite indifferent to the treasure hunter's poaching. That rather irked the lady. I wonder… Interesting creature, Sydes. Has a mental quirk. He put his finger on it, too. A collector! Just that… But Bassett. Not a nice person. Worries old Rexon. Carlotta feels it, too. Something familiar about those cold eyes. Queer. And why should he pretend about Oberlachen? No ski runs or toboggan slides there. Only a lake and a castle and a few peasants. Probably never been there. He met Richard at Saint Moritz. He would. And when I mentioned Amsterdam, Jacques wasn't having any. Well, well… No, Van. As I said. A dizzy lot. Social life at its gaudiest. Too much mental makeup."

He brought out his *Régie* cigarettes, lighted one, and stretched his legs.

"And all through the evening I kept thinking of little Ella Gunthar. Natural and fresh. Lovely. However…"

# CHAPTER FOUR

## *The First Murder*

*(Thursday, January 16; 8 a.m.)*

**THE NEXT MORNING** at eight there was excited knocking at our door.

"Mr. Vance! Mr. Vance!" I recognized the old butler's voice. "Mr. Rexon says will you please come to the den at once, sir."

Vance jumped up. "What's wrong, Higgins?"

"I—I don't know."

"Right!"

He dressed speedily, and we went into the hall. A woman, in the black livery of a housekeeper, was bent over the railing of the stairs. She heard us and backed against the wall, eyes staring, body rigid. Vance halted, looked at her sharply. She was tall, well built, about forty. She had green eyes, black hair, a cryptic face. A superior woman, but over-taut.

"Could you hear?" Vance's tone was cold.

"There's tragedy!" she said, in a tense, contralto voice.

"Common commodity of life. Relax."

We hurried downstairs.

"The Manor's strangest creature so far," Vance remarked to me. "Inhibited. Menacing. Knows too much. Volcanic. But only smouldering. *She's* tragedy. God help her..."

Carrington Rexon was in a house gown. With him in the den was a huge middle-aged man in a lumberjacket, corduroy trousers, and laced leather boots. He was pale and nervous. There was sweat on his hands as he steadied himself against the mantel.

"Eric Gunthar here, my overseer," Rexon told us, "just found the body of Lief Wallen in Tor Gulch near here. He's evidently fallen from the ledge on top. Gunthar came in to report to me and get aid. Would you go with him, Vance? I've already phoned for the doctor... Wallen was the guard of the Manor's west wing, where the Gem Room is."

"An indication perhaps. Quite. I understand. Gladly."

"Lief must have slipped," Gunthar put in thickly.

"Be sure you have someone replace him tonight," ordered Rexon. "Better take a couple of men to bring him up," he added.

"Darrup's down at the lower rink. I'll find another." Gunthar's hand brushed his forehead. "Wallen was a bad sight, Squire... Can I have another drink—?"

"You've had too much already," snapped Vance. "Move!"

Gunthar led the way sullenly. As we crossed the main road just before the house, a strange shabby figure appeared. A straggly white beard accentuated his stooped shoulders. He shuffled as he walked, but there was wiry energy in his movements. He turned quickly toward a clump of trees, as if to avoid us. Gunthar hailed him peremptorily.

"Come here, Jed. We need you." The old man shuffled up obediently. "Lief's gone over the crags at Tor Gulch. We'll be bringing him up."

The old man grinned childishly. For some reason the tragedy seemed to amuse him. "Maybe you're drinking too much, Eric. Ella said you struck her last week. You shouldn't do that. The Gulch'll hold more'n one."

We picked up Guy Darrup, the estate carpenter. Gunthar explained. Darrup's eyes clouded. There was unfriendliness in them. As we headed westward down the path he said: "I guess that'll make your job safe for a while now, Mr. Gunthar."

Gunthar snarled. "Get on. Mind your own business. Maybe *you'd* like to be overseer?"

"I'd do everyone fair." There was bitterness in the remark.

We took a circuitous route to the base of the rocky crags, passed through a cluster of trees over which the mist hung. We went north across a frozen stream, then turned in the general direction from which we came.

"You're Miss Ella's father, aren't you, Gunthar?" Vance spoke for the first time.

Gunthar gave an affirmative grunt.

"Who's *he*?" With a move of the head Vance indicated the old man shuffling briskly far ahead.

A sudden decision prompted ingratiation on Gunthar's part. "Old Jed. He was overseer here before me. Pensioned off now. He's cracked. Lives alone down in the Green Glen—named it himself. Doesn't mingle. We call him the Green Hermit... Nasty business about Lief, with the house full of guests—"

"That remark of Darrup's. Is there talk of a new overseer?"

"Hell! They're always talking. I make 'em work. They don't like it."

Old Jed turned abruptly to the right past an eruption of shrubs.

"Hey," bawled Gunthar, "how do *you* know where to go?"

"I reckon I know where Lief is," Jed cackled. He disappeared behind a projecting rock.

"He's cracked," Gunthar repeated.

"Thanks for the information." As Vance spoke a shout came from Old Jed.

"Here's Lief, Eric."

We came up. A crumpled body, hideously twisted, lay at the foot of a stone cliff. The face was torn and clotted, and the bare head was violently misshapen. There was a dark pool of coagulated blood.

Vance leaned over the figure, examined it closely; then he stood up. "No doctor can help. We'll leave him here. Darrup'll watch. I'll phone Winewood." He looked up at the cliffside and then through the trees at the Manor towers beyond.

Gunthar waved Old Jed away.

"You really oughtn't strike Ella, Eric," the old man admonished with a faint grin as he moved off round the cliffs to the flat meadow.

"Can we get to the top of the cliff on our way back to the Manor?" asked Vance.

Gunthar hesitated. "There's a steep short cut back a ways. But it's a dangerous climb—"

"We'll take it. Get going."

When we had struggled up the slippery, treacherous incline, Gunthar indicated the approximate spot where Lief Wallen must have gone over. There were shrub oaks near the edge of the cliff and Vance moved among them, gazing down at the thin layer of crusted snow. Suddenly he knelt beside a sturdy tree bole. "Blood, Gunthar." He pointed to an irregular dark patch a few inches from the tree trunk.

Gunthar sucked in his breath. "Holy God—up here!"

"Oh, quite." Vance rose. "No. No accident. Too bad the wind last night obliterated the tale of footprints. However... We'll be going. Work to do."

Gunthar halted abruptly. "Old Jed knew just where the body was!"

"Thanks awfully." Vance hastened down the long slope toward the Manor.

# CHAPTER FIVE

## *The Curse of the Emeralds*

*(Thursday, January 16; 9:30 a.m.)*

CARRINGTON REXON WAS drinking his coffee in the den when we returned.

"Up to the police," Vance announced. Then he explained... "I'll phone Winewood." He went to the telephone and conversed briefly.

Rexon rang. Higgins entered.

"Oh! Ah!" Vance sat down. "Many thanks. Just coffee, Higgins." He lighted a cigarette with unusual deliberation and stretched his legs before him.

Rexon was silent, coldly calm. He studied Vance over his coffee cup.

"Sorry you should be bothered," he murmured. "I was hoping my anxiety was unwarranted."

"One never knows, does one, old friend? We do our best."

Lieutenant O'Leary, of the Winewood police, a tall, shrewd and capable man, far superior to the ordinary country constable, arrived simultaneously with Doctor Quayne.

"Sorry, doctor. No need for you." Vance gave the details. "Fellow's been dead for hours, I'd say. It's the Lieutenant's problem."

"Doctor Quayne is our official physician," said O'Leary.

"Ah!" Vance threw his cigarette in the grate. "That facilitates matters. We'll go down at once. Darrup's watching the body. I ordered it left where Gunthar found it. Forgive my intrusion, Lieutenant. Sole interest Mr. Rexon."

"Quite correct, sir," O'Leary returned. "We'll see how the land lies."

"It lies exceeding black despite the snow."

Ten minutes later Doctor Quayne was examining Lief Wallen's body.

"A long fall," he commented. "Battered badly by the impact. Been dead all of eight hours. Poor Wallen. An honest, conscientious chap."

"That linear depression and laceration above the right ear," Vance suggested.

Quayne leaned over the body again for several moments. "I see what you mean." He looked up at Vance significantly. "I'll know more after the autopsy." He rose, frowning. "That's all now, Lieutenant. I'll be getting along—I've several calls to make."

"Thank you, doctor." O'Leary spoke courteously. "I'll attend to the routine."

Quayne bowed and departed.

O'Leary looked at Vance shrewdly. "What about that depression and laceration, sir?"

"Come with me a moment, Lieutenant." And Vance led the way to the cliff above. He pointed to the dark stain by the shrub-oak bole.

O'Leary inspected it and nodded slowly. Then he gave Vance a steady look. "What's your theory, sir?"

"Must I? But it's only a vague idea, Lieutenant. Highly illusory. That bash on Wallen's head might be from an instrument. Doesn't fit with a tumble. The poor johnnie could have been hit elsewhere and shoved over the cliff to cover up. There are faint indications in the snow hereabouts, despite last night's wind. Remote speculation at best. But there could have been three people here last night. Marks not clear. No. Proof lackin'... My theory? Wallen was struck near the Manor. Struck over the ear with an instrument shaped—let us say—like the blunt end of a spanner. His skull was fractured. Then he was dragged here. Two faint lines up the slope. Heels, perhaps. The body was dropped to the ground here so the other could hold to this tree while shoving Wallen over the cliff. Hemorrhage from the nose and ears intervened. Hence the blood here."

"I don't like it, sir." O'Leary frowned glumly.

"Neither do I. You asked for it."

O'Leary looked down at the telltale stain, then back at Vance. "You'll help us, sir? I'd be flattered. No need pretending I don't know of you."

"Disregardin' the compliment, I'd be happy to." Vance took out a cigarette. "My sole interest Mr. Rexon. As I said."

"I understand. My thanks. I'll get the machinery going." O'Leary strode off briskly.

When we returned to the Manor the sun was streaming into the spacious glass-enclosed veranda which stretched across the entire east side of the house. At the foot of a short terrace leading from the veranda was a large artificially controlled skating rink, lined on three sides with slender trees and landscaped gardens. Immediately below, to the south, was a pleasant pavilion.

Joan Rexon reclined on the veranda in a tufted wheelchair built like a *chaise longue*; and beside her in a small wicker porch chair sat Ella Gunthar. Vance joined them with a smile of greeting. Joan Rexon was frail and wistful, but she gave little impression of invalidism. Only the blue veins in her slender hands indicated the long illness which had sapped her strength since childhood.

"Isn't it terrible, Mr. Vance!" Ella Gunthar said in a quavering voice. He looked at her a moment questioningly. "My father has just told us about poor Lief Wallen. You know, don't you?"

Vance nodded. "Yes. But we mustn't let that cast a shadow over us here." He smiled to Joan.

"It's very difficult to avoid it," Miss Rexon said. "Lief was so kind and thoughtful..."

"The more reason not to think of such things," Vance declared.

Ella Gunthar nodded seriously. "The sunshine and the snow—there *are* happy things in the world to think about." She placed her hand tenderly over Joan's. But the thought of the tragedy remained with her as well. "Poor Lief must have fallen on his way home this morning."

Vance looked at her meditatively. "No. Not this morning," he said. "It was last night—around midnight."

Ella gripped her chair, and a frightened look came into her eyes. "Midnight," she breathed. "How terrible!"

"Why do you say that, Miss Ella?" The girl's manner puzzled Vance.

"I—I—At midnight..." Her voice trailed off.

Vance quickly turned the conversation, but failed to alter the girl's strange mood. At length he excused himself and went into the house. He had barely reached the foot of the main stairs when a hand was placed on his arm. Ella Gunthar had followed him.

"Are you sure it was—midnight?" Her whisper was tense and pleading.

"Somewhere thereabouts." Vance spoke lightly. "But why are you so upset, my dear?"

Her lips trembled. "I saw Lieutenant O'Leary come in with you and go toward Mr. Rexon's den. Tell me, Mr. Vance, why is he here? Is anything—wrong? Will we all have to go to Winewood—to answer questions maybe?"

Vance laughed reassuringly. "Please don't trouble your lovely little head. There'll be an inquest, of course—it's the law, y' know. Just formality. But they'll certainly not ask you to go."

Her eyes opened very wide. "An inquest?" she repeated softly. "But I want to go. I want to hear—everything."

Vance was nonplused. "Aren't you being foolish, child? Run back and read to Joan and forget all about—"

"But you don't understand." She caught her breath sharply. "I've *got* to go to the inquest. Maybe—" She turned suddenly and hurried back to the veranda.

"My word!" murmured Vance. "What can possibly be in that child's mind?"

On the upper landing, as we turned toward our rooms, the housekeeper stepped out unexpectedly from a small corridor. She drew herself up mysteriously.

"He's dead, isn't he?" Her tone was sepulchral. "And perhaps it wasn't an accident."

"How could one know?" Vance was evasive.

"Normal things don't happen here," she ran on tensely. "Those emeralds have put a curse on this house—"

"You've been reading the wrong novels."

She ignored the implication. "Those green stones—they create an atmosphere. They attract. They send forth temptation. They radiate fire."

Vance smiled. "What do you find abnormal here?"

"Everything. Darling Joan is an invalid. Old Jed's a fanatical mystic. Miss Naesmith brings strange people here. There's intrigue and deep jealousies everywhere. Mr. Rexon wants to choose his son's wife." She smiled inscrutably. "He doesn't know he's building on sand. It all started years ago."

"You hear much, what?" Vance spoke satirically.

"And I see much. The Rexon dynasty is falling. Young Mr. Richard pretends much; but the first night he got back from Europe a girl was waiting for him in the rear hall back of the stairs. He took her in his arms without a word and he held her close and long." She came nearer and lowered her voice. "It was Ella Gunthar!"

"Really, now." Vance laughed indifferently. "Young love. Any objection?"

The woman turned angrily and went down the hall.

# CHAPTER SIX

## *A Woman's Barb*

*(Thursday, January 16; 4:30 p.m.)*

VANCE DESERTED THE Manor an hour later, just as the noonday siren shrilled overhead, the surrounding hills catching the note and throwing the echo back and forth much longer than the original blast warranted. Carrington Rexon had long taken a boyish delight in retaining this outmoded signal for his workmen. He admitted it served no purpose, but it amused him to continue to use it.

The early winter dusk had begun to fall when Vance returned.

"Been snoopin' and talkin' round the estate," he told Carrington Rexon, settling himself comfortably before the fire. "Much needed activity. Hope you don't mind."

Rexon's laugh was mirthless. "I only hope your time wasn't wasted."

"No. Not wasted. I'll be frank. You want it, I know."

Rexon nodded stiffly.

"Things not happy," summarized Vance. "Meanness at work. And jealousies. Nothing overt. Just undercurrents. They could erupt, however. Gunthar's hard on the men. That doesn't help... Hear you've been planning to replace him as overseer. Wallen mentioned. Any truth in that?"

"Frankly, yes. But I was in no hurry."

"Lief Wallen wanted to marry Ella. Both father and daughter protested. Friction—scenes. Not nice. Much bitterness. Source of general resentment of estate workers toward Miss Ella. Think she considers herself superior to the rest of them because she's Miss Joan's companion. Only Old Jed defends her. They answer he has delusions and a soft spot for the color green. Implication bein' the presence of the emeralds has affected him. Everyone adding fuel to a smoulderin' fire and waiting for a flareup."

Rexon chuckled. "And perhaps you think, Vance, that I, too, am affected with the rest."

Vance made a deprecating motion. "By the by, yours is the only key to the Gem Room, what?"

"Good Heavens, yes! Special key and special lock. And a steel door."

"Been in the room today?"

"Oh, yes. Everything's quite in order."

Vance changed the subject. "Tell me about your housekeeper."

"Marcia Bruce? Solid as rock."

"Yes. I believe you. Honest, but hysterical."

Rexon chuckled again. "You've noticed much... But she adores Joan—cares for her like a mother when Ella Gunthar is off duty. Basically, Bruce is a fine woman. Quayne agrees. There's a fellow-feeling between those two. She was superintendent of nurses in a hospital once. Quayne's a worthy man, too. I'm glad to see that friendship developing."

"Ah!" Vance smiled. "I perceive Squire Rexon is sentimental."

"The human heart desires happiness for others as well as for oneself." Rexon was serious now. "What else did you learn, Vance? Anything pertaining to Lief Wallen's death?"

Vance shook his head. "Solution may come through irrelevancies. Later. I've only begun." Then he went out to the drawing room.

Bassett sat at the table near the veranda door where we first met him. He had just reached up and caught Ella Gunthar's arm as she passed. He was smirking up at her unpleasantly. She drew away from him. Bassett let her go. "Haughty, aren't we?" His eyes followed her with a sardonic leer as she returned to Miss Joan.

Vance strolled up. "Not skiing today, Mr. Bassett? Thought the whole jolly crowd was up on the Winewood trails."

"I slept too late and missed the party... Pretty blond thing, that Ella Gunthar." His eyes drifted back to the veranda. "Unusually attractive for a servant."

Vance's eyes narrowed, hard as steel, and drew Bassett's gaze. "We're all servants. Some to our fellow men. Some to our vices. Think that over." He went out to the veranda.

Lieutenant O'Leary was just coming up the steps at the side entrance.

"Doctor Quayne's doing the autopsy now," he announced. "Inquest tomorrow at noon. You'll have to attend, I'm afraid, sir. I'll pick you up."

"Any complications ahead?" asked Vance.

"No. I've soft-pedaled everything. John Brander, our coroner, is a good man. He likes Rexon. And I've explained the situation. He won't ask embarrassing questions."

"Accident verdict, maybe?"

"I hope so, sir. Brander understands. It'll give us time."

"A pleasure to work with you, Lieutenant."

O'Leary went inside to see Rexon, and Vance strode to where Joan and Ella Gunthar were sitting.

A noisy group of guests, returning from their skiing expedition, came clattering up the terrace, passed us with cheery greetings, and continued upstairs. Carlotta Naesmith and Stanley Sydes remained on the veranda and joined us.

Ella Gunthar was looking about anxiously.

"It's really no use, Ella," Miss Naesmith told her satirically. "Dick's gone daffy over Sally Alexander."

"I don't believe it!"

Miss Naesmith's mouth twisted in a cruel smile. "Does it hurt, Ella?"

"Carlotta! Cat!" There was no mirth in Sydes' reprimand.

"How do you feel today, Joan?" Miss Naesmith's mood changed as the girl smiled up sweetly. "And you, too, Mr. Vance. Why didn't you join the skiing party? It was glorious. At least ten inches of powder over a deep base."

"Isn't there enough snow already, in these locks of mine?"

"And most becoming, Sir Galahad!" She turned and stroked Sydes' temple. "Wonder if Stan'll be handsome when he gets grey."

"I promise you, Goddess," declared Sydes, "I'll be unutterably fascinating." He leaned over her. "And now, for the last time—"

"I always get seasick. I'll seek my treasure nearer home."

"Maybe I will too, if you spurn my invitation." Sydes' tone was fretful and aggressive.

"What do you think this wild man wants, Joan?" Miss Naesmith explained banteringly. "He insists I sail with him to Cocos Island and go diving for the treasure of the *Mary Dear* in Wafer Bay."

"Oh, that would be wonderful!" There was pathetic longing in Joan Rexon's voice.

"You dear, sweet child." The older girl's tone softened. Then she went upstairs, and Sydes followed.

A while later Marcia Bruce came out. "You may run along home, Ella. I'll take our darling in charge."

Vance rose.

"And I'll see Miss Ella home."

I knew he had great compassion for the girl who had no part in the gay sophisticated life about her. And I knew why he wished to walk with her to her father's cottage. He would strive to cheer and amuse her, so that the sting of Miss Naesmith's words might be forgot.

# CHAPTER SEVEN

## *The Inquest*

*(Friday, January 17; noon.)*

THE CORONER'S INQUEST increased the tension of the situation. Ella Gunthar had spoken urgently to Vance as soon as she arrived at the Manor that morning. She was fully cognizant of the time and place of the inquest and determined to be there. Vance sought to dissuade her, but finally abandoned the effort. He realized there was some deeper reason than mere curiosity, and arranged to take her with us in O'Leary's car.

At the bend in the roadway where it joined the main highway O'Leary signaled sharply on his horn. The sound found a prolonged echo in the archaic midday siren reverberating over the estate and weirdly following us like a mechanical nemesis as we drove on. The Lieutenant offered assurances to Vance's unvoiced concern.

"It won't take us more than ten minutes to get there. Brander'll wait for us."

The small room in the Town Hall at Winewood was well filled with townspeople and workers from the Rexon estate; but there were no guests from the Manor itself.

At one end of the room on a low platform was a long table at which a heavy-set, red-faced man with blinking eyes presided.

"That's John Brander," whispered O'Leary. "A reasonable man. Local real-estate lawyer."

At the left of the table, partitioned off by a railing, sat the jury, simple and honest men of the conventional type one would expect to find in a country town. A constable, with an ineffectual air of importance, stood beside the witness stand.

Eric Gunthar was called first. He explained briefly how he had come upon Lief Wallen's body on his way to work, and had returned to the Gulch with Old Jed, Darrup and Vance. Under adroit questioning, his trip to the summit of the cliff with Vance was brought out; but when Gunthar became too voluble regarding the blood spot, he was somewhat abruptly dismissed, and Darrup was called. He appeared cowed and had little to add to Gunthar's testimony. Old Jed proved a somewhat pathetic figure on the witness stand, and Brander wasted no time on him.

Vance was called next. Brander's questions elicited largely repetitions of the testimony already given; and despite the coroner's obvious attempt at caution, the blood stain by the scrub oak on the cliff was necessarily gone into at considerable length. Brander seemed to attach no particular importance to it and contrived a subtle suggestion that the blood might have been other than human blood. I myself was conscious of a fleeting mental image of some boy or amateur huntsman shooting a rabbit scurrying over the snow.

"Were there footprints anywhere near the spot?" Brander asked.

"No. No footprints," Vance answered. "There were, however, vague impressions in the snow."

"Anything definite?"

"No." And Vance was permitted to step down.

Doctor Quayne was then sworn in. His dignity and soft manner were impressive. The jury listened with patent respect. The doctor's testimony was perfunctory and technical. He told of the condition of the body when he first saw it; estimated the time of death; and hastened over the findings of the autopsy. He emphasized, however, the peculiar skull wound over Wallen's right ear.

"Now, this skull wound, doctor," the coroner interposed. "Just what was peculiar about it?"

"It was somewhat sharply outlined and depressed, running from the right ear for about four inches toward the temple—not exactly what one would expect from even violent contact with a flat surface."

"There was snow where Wallen struck?"

"About an inch, I should say."

"Did you examine the ground under the snow for a possible projection?"

"No. It would have been visible had it been there."

"But there are projecting rocks on the cliff between the upper ledge and the ground, aren't there?"

"Slight ones. Yes."

"Is it not possible, then, Wallen's head glanced one of these rocks in falling?"

Doctor Quayne pursed his lips. He expressed considerable doubt.

"However," persisted Brander, "you couldn't say definitely—could you, doctor—that this particular injury was wholly incompatible with the fall?"

"No. I couldn't say that definitely. I merely state that the injury seemed strange in the circumstances; one hardly to be expected."

"But still,"—Brander leaned forward with marked courtesy—"you'll pardon me, doctor, if I insist on the point. Such an injury would have been *possible* in an accidental fall from the cliff?"

"Yes,"—Doctor Quayne's tone showed annoyance—"it would have been possible."

"That will be all, doctor. Thank you for your clarity and help."

O'Leary was then called. His testimony, brief and businesslike, served merely to corroborate that of preceding witnesses. As he stepped down there came an unexpected and dramatic interlude. Guy Darrup suddenly leaped to his feet.

"You ain't doin' fair to Lief Wallen, Mr. Brander," he shouted righteously. "You ain't askin' for the things where truth lies. I could tell you—"

Brander struck the table with his gavel. "If you have evidence to give," he said with acerbity, "you should have stated it when you were on the stand."

"You didn't ask me the right questions, you didn't, Mr. Brander. I know plenty about poor Lief."

"Swear him in again, Constable."

"Not comfortin' for us," whispered Vance to O'Leary.

"Brander has no choice." O'Leary, too, was apprehensive.

Darrup took the oath a second time.

"Now give us your withheld evidence, Darrup." Brander's biting tone was wasted.

"Maybe you don't know, Mr. Brander, the queer wrong things that goes on over there at the Squire's." Darrup spoke like a zealot aroused. "Mr. Gunthar's always a-bullyin'. An' he drinks too much to suit the Squire. He's been warned, he has. An' it was Lief Wallen that was gonna step in his boots—just like *he* stepped in Old Jed's boots. An' Lief wanted to marry that pretty girl of his—the one down there who looks after Miss Joan." Ella Gunthar drew back as he pointed. "Lief had a right. He'da made her a good honest husband. But Mr. Gunthar didn't want it. I guess he's got his own ideas." Darrup contorted his lips into a shrewd smile. "An' the girl didn't want it neither. She thinks she's better than us. An' there's been plenty o' trouble about it all—Lief wasn't a boy who'd give up easy..."

Darrup breathed noisily, and hurried on.

"But that ain't all, Mr. Brander—not by a long ways. Nothing's right up there at the Squire's. There's funny things goin' on. Deep, dark things—things you ain't taught about in the Bible. What's the girl doin' down in the Green Glen at night times, I'd like to know? I've seen her sneakin' to Old Jed's hut. There's plottin'. Everybody's lyin'. Everybody's hatin'. An' Old Jed's queer. He don't talk to nobody. But he's up to something, always lookin' up at the trees, an' lettin' the stream water run through his fingers, like a kid. An' then, just when young Lief's about to step into Mr. Gunthar's job, he goes an' falls off the cliff. Lief knew his way about the grounds better'n to do that. Anyway, what's he doin' up there that time o' night when he's supposed to be watchin' round the Manor?"

Brander's patience gave out. His gavel smashed down.

"Did you come here to vent your hates, man? That's not evidence. That's old women's talk."

*"Not evidence!"* shrieked Darrup. "Then ask Mr. Gunthar's girl why she was runnin' down the slope from the cliff at twelve o'clock that night when Lief *fell over*!"

"What's that?"

"You heard me, you did, Mr. Brander. I was workin' late in the pavilion, fixin' things for the Squire's party. An' here she comes runnin' down the slope an' turned right by the pavilion. An' she was cryin', too."

I looked at Ella Gunthar. Her face was white, her lips trembled. There was a subdued commotion in the room. Brander hesitated, looked uneasy. He rustled through some papers before him. Then he looked angrily at Darrup.

"Your statements are irrelevant." He paused. "Unless, perhaps,"—there was jocularity in his tone—"you're accusing a mere girl of hurling a big fellow like Wallen over the cliff. Is that what you mean?"

"No, Mr. Brander." Darrup lapsed again into sullenness. "It wasn't her as could've done it. I'm only tellin' you—"

Again the gavel descended. "That's enough! This inquest is not for the purpose of injuring a young woman's reputation. It is merely to establish by what means Wallen came to his death, and, if by criminal means, at whose hand. Your speculations are, therefore, not helpful to this investigation. Step down, Darrup." Darrup obeyed, and Brander turned quickly to O'Leary. "Any more witnesses, Lieutenant?"

O'Leary shook his head.

"That's all then." Brander spoke briefly to the jury. They filed out. In less than half an hour their verdict was announced:

"We find that Lief Wallen met his death by an accidental fall, under suspicious circumstances."

Brander was startled. He opened his mouth, was about to speak, but said nothing. The inquest was over.

"There's a verdict!" O'Leary scoffed to Vance as we drove back to the Manor. "No sense whatever. But Brander did his best."

"Yes—oh, yes. Not strictly legal, perhaps. Could have been worse. However..."

Ella Gunthar sat in the corner of the back seat beside me, a handkerchief pressed to her mouth, staring, unseeing, over the quiet winter landscape.

Vance took her gently in hand when we arrived. "Was Darrup telling the truth, my dear?" he asked.

"I don't know what you mean..."

"Were you running down the slope that night?"

"I—No. Of course not." She raised her chin defiantly. "I was at home at midnight. I didn't hear anything..."

"Why are you fibbing?" he asked sternly. She compressed her lips and said nothing. Vance went on with tenderness. "Maybe I know. You're a brave little soldier. But very foolish. Nothing's going to hurt you. I want you to trust me." He held out his hand.

Her eyes searched his face a moment. A faint smile showed on her lips. Then she placed her hand confidently in his.

"Now run along to Joan—and let that smile come all the way out."

# CHAPTER EIGHT

## *Secret Plans*

*(Friday, January 17; evening.)*

THAT EVENING, SHORTLY after dinner, I stood with Vance on the veranda, looking out over the shadows on the skating rink. Echoes of music and gaiety drifted out to this secluded corner from the drawing room. Vance was in a serious, contemplative mood and smoked a *Régie* in silence, with a faraway expression.

Before long, however, there was the sound of approaching footsteps behind us, and Vance turned to greet Carlotta Naesmith.

"Brooding over your sins, Sir Knight?" the girl asked as she came up. "It really doesn't help. I've tried it… I sought you out to ask a most important question—tu-whit, tu-who: Do you skate gracefully?"

"At my time of life!" Vance pretended dejection. "But your query's flatterin'. I'm duly grateful."

"I was hoping you did skate. We do so need a Master of Ceremonies." She prodded him playfully. "You are hereby elected."

"It sounds interestin'. Explanat'ry instructions in order."

"It's like this," Miss Naesmith readily complied. "All the inmates of the zoo, barring the decrepit, are throwing a party for Richard tomorrow night. A sort of farewell celebration. It's to be on the rink out there… I'm hostess *pro tem*, you know. Originality expected from one so brilliant. Hence skates—that being the best idea the brain could conjure up."

"Sounds jolly," said Vance. "And my duties?"

"Oh, just to keep things going. Be officious—you can. Announce the animals. I'm sure you get it: every animal act has a ringmaster."

"Must I supply liniment?"

"You wrong us, sir!" she chirped indignantly. "We all skate amazingly well. I understand the bar will be temporarily padlocked."

"That could help, y' know." Vance smiled.

"We're planning it quite seriously," she ran on. "We're even going to practice on the lower rink tomorrow. And we're going to Winewood in the morning to scout for costumes… Sounds a bit horrible, doesn't it?"

"Oh, no!" Vance protested. "Sounds jolly. As I said." He looked at the girl searchingly. "Tell me, Miss Naesmith, why did you try to hurt Ella Gunthar yesterday?"

Miss Naesmith's mood changed. Her eyes narrowed. She shrugged noncommittally.

"It doesn't take both my eyes to see that she and Dick are attracted to each other. They always were as kids."

"And Sally Alexander?"

She laughed without mirth. "Dick didn't speak to her all day. But let Ella worry."

"And it doesn't take both my eyes"—Vance did not shift his gaze—"to see that you will never pine away if Richard is diverted."

She pondered that a moment. "Dick's a nice boy. It's Papa Rexon's idea, you know. And who am *I* to upset his fondest dream?"

"Is it nice to be bitter?" Vance brought out his cigarettes. Miss Naesmith accepted one, and he lighted one himself.

"Oh, it's done in the best circles," the girl said facetiously. "And anyway, it's not the man's place to walk out. That's *my* prerogative."

"I see. Mere technique of etiquette at fault. Well, well."

The girl blew Vance a kiss and went back to the noisy drawing room.

"As I thought," he murmured, as if to himself. "Neither wants it. Richard makes the fact evident. *Ergo*, pique. Evinced by a display of cruelty. Ancient feminine sequence. However, nice girl at heart. It'll all arrange itself. Poor papa. Yes, the Rexon dynasty is crumblin'. Same like Bruce predicts." He looked out over the shadowy rink, drawing deeply on his *Régie*. "Come, I've a wishful idea." He spoke irrelevantly as he turned suddenly and went inside.

We found Joan Rexon in her own sitting room across the hall. She was on a divan by the window, and Marcia Bruce was reading to her.

"Why aren't you in the drawing room, young lady?" Vance asked pleasantly.

"I'm resting tonight," the girl replied. "Carlotta told me there's to be a big party for Dick tomorrow night, and I want to feel well, so I won't miss any of it."

Vance sat down. "Would it tire you too much if I talked to you a few minutes?"

"Why, no. I'd love it."

Vance turned to Miss Bruce. "Mind if I speak with Miss Joan alone?"

The housekeeper rose in resentful dignity and went to the door. "More mystery." Her tone was hollow. Her green eyes flashed.

"Oh, quite," laughed Vance. "A dark plot, in fact. But I can complete my dire machinations in ten minutes. Come back then, what? There's an angel."

The woman went without a word.

"I want to talk a moment about Ella." Vance drew up his chair beside the slight reclining figure of Joan Rexon.

"Dear Ella," the girl said sweetly.

"She is a dear, isn't she?... I've wondered since I've been here why I never see her on the rink. Doesn't she skate?"

Joan Rexon smiled sadly. "Oh, she used to love skating. But I guess she's lost her interest—since I fell."

"But I know you love to see others skating and being happy."

She nodded. "I do. I do. I've never forgot what fun I used to have myself. That's why Dad kept up the rinks and the pavilion. So I can sit on the veranda and watch the others. He often brings famous skaters up here just to perform for me."

"He'd do anything he thought would make you happy," said Vance.

She nodded again, emphatically. "And so would Ella... You know, Mr. Vance, I'm really a very lucky girl. And I do have wonderful times just watching others do the things I'd love to do."

"That's why I thought Miss Ella might be doing your skating for you, so to speak."

The girl turned her head slowly toward the window. "Maybe I'm to blame, Mr. Vance. I've often thought that."

"Tell me about it," Vance urged softly.

"Well, you see, when I was a little girl, just after my accident, Ella went out on the rink and skated—she was a beautiful skater. I watched her and I was very selfish, I think. Just the sight of her skating seemed to hurt me. I don't exactly understand it. I was such a baby. It—it—"

"I understand, my dear."

"And when Ella came back to the veranda I was crying... After that, for several years, I saw Ella only at intervals. She was at school, you know. And we never spoke again about her skating."

Vance took her hand gently. "She was probably too busy with other things to keep up her skating. Or perhaps she lost interest because you couldn't join her. You needn't feel guilty... But it wouldn't hurt you any more, would it?"

"Oh, no." She forced a smile. "I wish she *would* skate again. I was just terribly foolish."

"We're all foolish when we're young." Vance laughed.

The girl nodded seriously. "I'm not foolish—that way—any more. Now when I see some wonderful skater I wish it were Ella. I know she could have done it."

"I know just how you feel." As he rose the door opened and Marcia Bruce entered.

"The plot's concocted," said Vance. "And I'm sure I haven't tired the young lady. She's quite ready to hear the ending of the story you were reading to her."

As we came out again into the hall and approached the stairway two figures stood conversing earnestly in a secluded nook at the rear. They were Carlotta Naesmith and Stanley Sydes. Vance merely glanced toward them and proceeded to the drawing room.

# CHAPTER NINE

## *An Abrupt Summons*

*(Saturday, January 18; forenoon.)*

THE NEXT MORNING Vance rose in good season and, after a hasty cup of coffee, left the house, alone, disappearing down the wide path which led past the pavilion to Gunthar's cottage. Shortly after his departure the other guests straggled down to the breakfast room and then assembled before the spacious gabled garage. One by one the cars were brought out and the cavalcade swung gaily up the hill to the main road and toward Winewood. Half an hour or so later the housekeeper piloted Joan Rexon tenderly to the now deserted veranda and with motherly attentions installed her on the specially built *chaise longue* near the windows overlooking the skating rink.

Barely was the girl settled when Vance and Ella Gunthar turned the corner of the path by the pavilion and came toward the house.

"You see, Miss Joan," Vance said as they entered, "not only do I see your charming companion home in the evening, but I escort her to you in the morning."

Ella Gunthar smiled. She seemed particularly happy. There was a new sparkle in her eyes. Marcia Bruce, apparently sensing something unusual, looked from Ella to Vance and back again. Then she rose, patted Joan Rexon fondly, and went indoors.

Vance remained on the veranda a while, chatting in his most trivial manner, and finally went inside to seek the comfort of the easy chair in his room. He seemed preoccupied and lay back, smoking listlessly for some time. His meditations, whatever they were, were interrupted by a knock on the door. Lieutenant O'Leary came in and sat down. There was an added sternness in his aquiline face.

"I wanted to see you alone, Mr. Vance. The butler said you were here, so I took the liberty..."

"Delighted, Lieutenant." Vance rearranged himself in his chair and lighted another *Régie*. "I trust you haven't brought disconsolate tidin's."

O'Leary fumbled with his pipe a moment without replying. When he got it going he looked up.

"I wonder, sir, if, by any chance, you have the same idea I have?"

"It could be." Vance's eyebrows went up questioningly. "What is your thought?"

"I'm convinced I know who killed Wallen."

Vance lay back lethargically and studied the strong set face of the man opposite.

"Amazin'!" he murmured. Then he shook his head. "No. No such thoughts here. Mind a blank as to that. Anyway, thanks for your confidence. Could you stretch it further?"

O'Leary, hesitant at first, now seemed eager to talk.

"I figure it this way, sir: I don't think Guy Darrup was lying at the inquest yesterday."

"No. Not lying. Merely impulsive and ingenuous. A simple honest mind ruled by zealous emotions. Indignations churned up in him, and boiled over."

"Then you believe him?"

"Oh, yes. Quite. No alternative. Fact is, I'd done a spot of spyin' around myself and already knew most of what he poured forth. Not a pleasant situation here and abouts. But where's it criminal? I need more guidance. Do you have it?"

"Here's how I've put it all together: Gunthar drinks too much and is about to be discharged. Wallen's slated for the promotion. That in itself is a good enough motive with rugged straightforward natures. Gunthar has just such a nature. He's not subtle, and apt to be cruel in his cups: he'd take the straight line—strong and forthright—when perplexed with a problem. Now, add to this motive the friction between him and Wallen regarding his daughter's future. Wouldn't you say that would set the stage?"

"Granted." Vance nodded. "Opportunity even simpler. But continue, Lieutenant."

"Exactly, sir. A fine opportunity. Gunthar knows the lay of the land. He knows Wallen's habits and knows his weaknesses. What could be easier for him than to inveigle Wallen to the cliff on some pretext, bash him over the head, and throw him over into the Gulch?... Miss Gunthar probably suspected her father's intent, followed him secretly up the cliff, and, when the thing was done, came running down, crying."

"And what could Gunthar hope to gain? asked Vance indifferently. "He would still be discharged."

"Oh, I know Wallen wasn't the only available man for the job. Rexon can get a dozen others, given a little time. But I gather Gunthar intended to give up his tippling—which is only of recent origin—and insinuate himself again into Rexon's good graces."

"But Gunthar was still drinking too much yesterday. I saw him both before and after the inquest."

"That substantiates my theory," O'Leary declared. "He needed it to buck him up—the experience is enough to undo a stronger man."

"True," conceded Vance. "The point fits snugly. What else, Lieutenant?"

"Gunthar threatened Wallen twice."

"Gossip?"

"Necessarily, of course. But I believe it's authentic enough. It'll be sworn to by reliable witnesses."

"A clever analysis, Lieutenant," drawled Vance. "But not a defense-proof case."

O'Leary showed resentment. "That's not all, sir." He pulled himself forward in his chair. "Gunthar can't prove a satisfactory alibi for the supposed time of the killing. He came into Murphy's tavern at Winewood at ten o'clock that night. He was nervous and drank more than usual. He left at about half-past eleven. It takes nearly half an hour to walk here from Winewood. An hour later Sokol, the druggist in Winewood, was driving home from a late party and saw Gunthar crossing the meadow on the far side of Tor Gulch. The man thought nothing of it at the time; but after the inquest he figured the information might have some bearing, and told me about it. True enough, Gunthar was headed for his cottage. But that isn't the short cut from Winewood. And it *is* the route he would have taken if he'd first been to the cliff... Does that strengthen my case against Gunthar?" finished O'Leary doggedly.

"Oh, markedly," Vance readily agreed. "All rather circumstantial, however, isn't it, Lieutenant?"

"That may be." There was a touch of bravado in his voice: a satisfying sense of triumph over Vance. "But sufficient grounds for arresting the man."

"Oh, tut, tut. I wouldn't do that." Vance was all mildness. "So far you've done exceeding well, Lieutenant. You put things together deuced cleverly. Why spoil it all by moving too precipitately? Tie a few more ends."

"I don't intend to act speedily. I could do with a few more facts."

"Exactly. A common need of mankind. I'll bear your theory in mind. Maybe I'll be able to supply the missing facts. Credit all yours."

O'Leary knocked out his pipe and rose. "I've several lines I'm following quietly. But I thought I'd tell you which way they're leading. I was hoping you might see things from my point of view."

"I do," Vance assured him. "You've done well. Thanks again for your confidence."

When O'Leary had shaken hands and gone, Vance crushed out his cigarette and walked to the window.

"Deuce take it, Van," he said, "the man's too specious. Speciousness. Curse of our modern age. He thinks straight, though. Competent chap. All for the best. Not a nice theory. I hope he's wrong."

An hour later Vance went below. The party that had driven off to Winewood earlier had returned. We saw some of them in the lower hall. From the drawing room came sounds indicating others there.

Doctor Quayne was sitting with Joan Rexon and Ella Gunthar on the veranda. He got up when he saw us and smiled.

"You come just in time, Mr. Vance," his pleasant voice greeted us. "Now you can entertain the young ladies. I'll have to run away in a few minutes to see some of my patients who need me much more than Joan does. I dropped by to make sure she was strong enough for the party tonight, and she doesn't need me at all. With the rest last night and this beautiful mild weather, she's all in readiness for the festivities."

"Anyway," Miss Rexon said, "I managed to keep you here an hour, doctor."

"That was purely social, my dear Joan." He turned back to Vance. "If all my patients were as charming as these two young ladies I'd never complete my rounds. The temptation to remain and visit would be greater than I could resist."

"Mr. Vance, is flattery supposed to be a cure?" Joan Rexon seemed very happy.

"There can be no flattery where you are concerned," Vance returned. "I know that Doctor Quayne means every word he says to you."

Several of the guests came out, joined us a moment to make a fuss over Joan Rexon, and then returned indoors. The midday siren sounded. Bassett, too, I noticed, strolled out; but he merely nodded and remained at the other end of the veranda. He sat down at a small table and began a game of solitaire.

The doctor glanced at his watch. "Good Heavens! That was the noon signal!" He gave the two girls a cordial bow. "You're both a corrupting influence." He went quickly through the drawing room door. A few minutes later we saw him drive away.

We remained on the veranda for another half hour, relaxing in the warm sunshine, and Vance entertained the girls with tales of his travels in Japan. In the midst of his engaging narrative he glanced toward the French doors just behind us. Excusing himself suddenly, he hastened toward the door. As he stepped inside he turned and beckoned me to follow.

Higgins was standing just by the entrance, his face like chalk, his watery old eyes bulging. Fear and horror pervaded his entire being as he clasped and unclasped his hands against his breast.

"Thank God you were here, Mr. Vance!" His voice quavered and the words were barely audible. "I couldn't find Mr. Richard. Come quickly, sir. Something terrible—" He moved swiftly toward the rear of the main stairs and led us to Carrington Rexon's den.

There, on the floor before the grate, lay the owner of Rexon Manor.

# CHAPTER TEN

## *The Missing Key*

*(Saturday, January 18; 12:30 p.m.)*

VANCE, DOWN ON one knee in a moment, cursorily examined the coagulating trickle of blood behind Carrington Rexon's right ear. He listened a moment to the labored breathing, then sought the pulse. He turned the man's face toward the light, found it ashen pale. He raised the upper eyelid of one eye; the eyeball was firm, the pupil contracted. He touched the cornea with his fingertip. The lids immediately compressed tightly.

"Not serious," Vance announced. "He's reacting now from unconsciousness... I say, Higgins, summon the doctor immediately." He loosened Rexon's collar and stock.

Higgins coughed.

"I phoned Doctor Quayne before I came out to you, sir. Fortunately, he was at home, sir. He should be here directly."

"Stout fella, Higgins. Now, if you'll call Lieutenant O'Leary—tell him to come here at once. Urgent. Explain, if necess'ry."

"Yes, sir." Higgins picked up the telephone, put through the call, and returned the receiver. "The Lieutenant says he'll be here in ten minutes, sir."

Vance stepped to the window and opened it. Then he went to the fireplace and added a fresh log. The crackling flames seemed to dissipate the gloom that hung over the room. A knock on the door was followed by the entry of Doctor Quayne, bag in hand.

"Good God! What's this!" He rushed to Rexon.

"Not too serious, doctor. No. Bad rap on the head." Vance moved away a step. "He should be coming to. Every indication of return of muscular tone. I found his pulse weak but regular. There was a definite corneal reflex when I opened his eye. Unmistakable resistance when I moved his head."

Quayne nodded and fussed with the wound. A low moan came from Rexon. His eyes opened, glazed, unseeing. At an order from Quayne, Higgins brought brandy. The doctor forced a stiff dose gently between Rexon's lips. The prostrate man moaned again and closed his eyes.

"Lucky I went home for lunch before continuing on my rounds..." The doctor chatted casually as he proceeded to examine Rexon. Finally he rose. "Everything quite in order," he finished cheerfully.

Rexon's eyes opened again, almost clear now. He recognized Vance and Quayne, attempted a smile, winced, and raised a hand to the back of his head.

"We'll take care of that in a moment." Quayne was kindly reassuring. Then, with Higgins' help, he placed Rexon on the sofa. With deft fingers he dressed the wound, continuing his assurances to the man.

While the doctor was thus busied, Lieutenant O'Leary came in. Vance, in a low tone, gave him the details.

"May we put a query or two now?" Vance asked as the doctor stepped away from the sofa.

"Certainly, certainly," Quayne told him. "Mr. Rexon'll be quite all right now."

Vance motioned Higgins from the room, and stepped to the sofa with O'Leary.

"Now, what can you tell us, old friend?" he asked.

"I doubt if I can tell you anything, Vance." Rexon's voice was low and husky, but it gained in volume as he continued. "I'd just risen from my desk to ring for Higgins... I must have been struck from behind." His hand moved to his head again. "The next thing I knew, you and Quayne were with me."

"Any idea how long ago that was?"

"Only a vague one, I'm afraid." Rexon thought a moment... "But wait! I think I heard the first notes of the siren before I lost consciousness... Yes. I'm positive. I recall being annoyed because it was so near twelve and my breakfast tray hadn't been removed. It's usually taken out of my way by eleven. That's why I was going to call Higgins."

"Had you been here in the den since you came down this morning, sir?" O'Leary put in.

"More or less, yes, Lieutenant. But I was out of the room for a few minutes once or twice."

"Had anyone been here with you?" asked Vance.

"Yes. Bruce came in for instructions, as she usually does when there are guests. And my son spent about a half hour with me. Doctor Quayne here stepped in to say hello before he went out to Joan. Sydes and Carlotta came in for a minute. Some of the other guests did, too. I'll try to think back, if you want to know who else."

"No—oh, no. Really doesn't matter." Vance stepped back.

"Do you recall any feeling of giddiness when you first rose to call Higgins?" the doctor asked. "Judging from the wound, I'd say it was highly possible you hit one of the fire irons as you fell."

"I don't see how," answered Rexon a bit nettled. "I wasn't dizzy. The sensation was I was struck from behind."

"Ah! I see," said Quayne thoughtfully.

Rexon suddenly started forward, his eyes averted frantically. A bunch of keys on a long chain dangled from his trousers pocket over the edge of the divan. He caught the keys and sank back, fumbling with them hysterically.

"The key!" he gasped after a moment. "The Gem Room key! God in Heaven! It's *gone!*"

"Easy now, Rexon," admonished the doctor. "It can't be gone. Look again—calmly."

Rexon ran his hands hopelessly through his pockets. O'Leary searched vainly on the floor. Vance stepped from the room, returning instantly to report that the Gem Room door was safely locked.

"Proves nothing!" exploded Rexon. "We must get in there at once. I'll get the duplicate key."

He rose feebly as he spoke, and moved unsteadily across the room. Snatching a priceless Rembrandt etching from the opposite wall, he threw it carelessly aside. Then he pressed a small wooden medallion, and a narrow panel shifted, revealing an oval steel plate with a dial and knob. His nervous fingers managed a sequence of turns—left and right and left again. Finally he pulled the plate open and reached inside the hidden wall safe. He brought out a key with a long slender shaft. Taking it from him, Vance led the way through the hall.

He had a little difficulty fitting the key into the lock, but finally succeeded and pushed the heavy steel door inward. Rexon brushed past him excitedly and came to a sudden stop in the middle of the famous Gem Room.

"They're gone!" His voice was little more than a hoarse whisper. "The most precious part of my collection. *And* Istar's—" His voice broke as he pointed spasmodically and began to sway.

Quayne stepped to him immediately, and took his arm. "My dear friend," he cautioned. He turned to us. "I'll take him back to the den, gentlemen." He led Rexon from the room.

Vance closed the door after the two men, and locked it. Lighting a cigarette, he moved leisurely through that interesting room, with O'Leary following him in silence. The room was completely void of furnishings except for the ebony carpet and the numerous metal-bound glass cases along the walls. Emeralds of various shapes and sizes, in exquisite and unique settings, were displayed against white velvet backgrounds. In the corner to which Rexon had pointed a case larger than the others had its front pane shattered. A smaller case beside the large one was similarly broken. Both were empty. But none of the other cases in the room seemed to have been disturbed.

"Very mystifyin'," Vance murmured. "Only two cases broken."

"Probably didn't have time; hurried job," suggested O'Leary.

"Quite, Lieutenant. All indications pointin' thus... Wonder what Istar has to do with it."

He stepped to the side window and forced the catch open. O'Leary looked on as he examined the heavy criss-cross iron bars that enclosed the entire window frame. Then they made a similar inspection of the other window.

"My word! Here's something interestin', Lieutenant. Bit of tamperin', what?" He directed O'Leary's attention to some peculiar ragged scratches across three of the bars.

O'Leary's brows went up. "Whoever it was must've tried this means of entry first and found it too cumbersome an undertaking. No patience."

"Or," returned Vance, "an interruption occurred. Aborted attempt. Could be. Let's toddle."

They reclosed the windows. Vance took another look about the room before unlocking the unwieldy door.

In the den Doctor Quayne was attempting futilely to console Rexon. "It's not as if they'd all been taken." Platitudes like that. "Only a few pieces..."

*"Only a few pieces!"* repeated Rexon despairingly. "The very pieces that matter! If they'd taken all the others and left me those—" He did not complete the sentence.

Vance handed Rexon the key. "I've relocked the door, of course. Now tell us just what is missing. And how is Istar mixed up in it?"

Rexon jerked himself up in his chair; leaned wearily against the desk. "Every unset stone I owned. Spent a lifetime collecting 'em."

"Those would be the easiest to dispose of, I take it," observed O'Leary respectfully.

"Yes. Exactly. A fortune for anyone into whose hands they came. All but the Istar..."

"Again, wherefore Istar?" persisted Vance.

"Queen Istar's necklace," groaned Rexon. "The rarest piece in my collection. From Egypt—eighteenth dynasty. It can never be replaced. Six high cabochon emeralds of flawless cut on a chain of smaller stones set in silver and pearls... You must remember it, Vance."

"Ah, yes. Of course," said Vance sympathetically. "Naughty queen—Istar. Always poppin' in and out to annoy folks."

O'Leary was making notes in a small book.

"When were you last in the room?" asked Vance.

"This morning, early. I go in every morning. Had Bruce there with me to do a little dusting. For the display to my guests this evening."

"Ah, yes. Very sad. Now, of course, there'll be no display."

"No." Rexon shook his head in keen disappointment.

"But the youngsters must have their party tonight as though nothing had happened. You agree, Rexon?" Vance's tone was significantly imperative.

"Yes, by all means," complied Rexon. "No need to upset everybody."

The doctor rose presently, picked up his bag. "You don't need my services any more just now, Rexon. Wish I could be more helpful. But I'll be back this evening to keep an eye on Joan for you."

"Thank you, Quayne. That's very good of you."

The doctor bowed himself out.

O'Leary closed his notebook. "Tell me, Mr. Rexon, was your overseer in to see you this morning?"

"Gunthar? No," replied Rexon. "He's probably been working on the rink and the pavilion all morning. But it's strange you should ask that. Higgins told me when I came down this morning that Gunthar had been here about half an hour earlier asking if he could see me. Higgins told him I wasn't down yet, and the man went away grumbling to himself. I don't understand it, for he never comes here unless I send for him."

O'Leary nodded with satisfaction. He stepped to the open window, lowered it and raised it again. Then he leaned out for a moment as if inspecting the flagging below. There was a speculative look in his eyes as he rejoined us.

In the hall Vance drew the Lieutenant aside. "What about Gunthar?" he asked in a low tone. "Any secrets to unbosom?"

"It's a clearer-cut case now than it was yesterday." The Lieutenant was solemn. "You admitted I had a good case then, sir. But add this to it: I tried to see Gunthar this morning. One of the workmen told me he had gone to the Manor to speak to the Squire. Seemed natural. So I waited around a while. But Gunthar didn't come back."

O'Leary cocked a triumphant eye at Vance.

"You see, sir, how easy it would have been for the man to have entered the den through the window, either then or later when Mr. Rexon was out of the room. He had only to wait back of the screen till the time was ripe. When he had struck the blow it would have been a moment's work for him to snatch the key and get to the Gem Room."

Vance nodded. "Deuced clever, Lieutenant. Logical from many points of view."

"Yes. And what's more," persisted O'Leary, "I'm not at all convinced his daughter Ella wasn't mixed up in it—you know, sir, like giving him the tip-off—"

"Oh, my dear fellow! You startle me no end. I say, aren't you carrying this prejudice against Gunthar a bit too far?"

O'Leary looked surprised that Vance apparently could not appreciate the circumstantial possibilities of the situation.

"No, I wouldn't say so," he retorted with the calmness of conviction. "I've got enough to arrest the girl along with her father."

"But on what grounds, Lieutenant?" Vance was concerned.

"As a material witness, if nothing else," was O'Leary's confident rejoinder.

Vance lighted a cigarette and blew a long ribbon of smoke. "Not attemptin' to try your case, Lieutenant. No. It's far too logical. Merely making an urgent request. Neither the girl nor papa is likely to run off tonight, what? Surely, tomorrow will serve your purpose quite as well. You'll wait, Lieutenant? I'm beggin'."

O'Leary studied Vance several moments. There was no denying the look of admiration beneath his perturbation and doubt. Finally he nodded. "I'll wait, sir. Though it goes against my best judgment." And he strode off across the veranda and disappeared down the side steps.

Vance, too, stepped out on the veranda a moment later. Joan Rexon still sat where we had left her, but Ella Gunthar was no longer there. In her place sat Carlotta Naesmith.

"My word!" murmured Vance. "No use hopin' the doughty Lieutenant didn't note Miss Ella's absence. No. Observin' fellow, O'Leary."

Bassett was still hunched over the table where he had started his game of Canfield. Stanley Sydes had joined him and sat in a chair opposite, acting as banker. A decanter of Bourbon stood between them.

# CHAPTER ELEVEN

## *Farewell Soirée*

*(Saturday, January 18; 9 p.m.)*

THE AFTERNOON HAD passed uneventfully. After lunch Carlotta Naesmith and Stanley Sydes invited Vance to go with the others and watch their practice routine on the ice. He had politely declined. Richard Rexon, who likewise remained at the Manor, had talked briefly with Vance regarding the stolen emeralds and spent the rest of the afternoon brooding about the matter. Miss Joan retired to her sitting room for a rest. The house was unusually quiet.

At dinner there was excited talk about the party. Especially were there mysterious hints of a surprise performer whom Mr. Rexon had invited for the occasion. No one seemed to have any specific information, however.

Dinner over, the older guests assembled on the veranda, grouping themselves on either side of Miss Joan's *chaise longue* at the center window. The night was clear and not too cold.

Shortly before nine Marcia Bruce brought Miss Joan out to her place.

"Please pull up a chair for Ella beside me," the girl requested. "She should be here any minute now."

Miss Bruce complied.

Doctor Quayne came up. After a word of encouragement to Miss Joan and a greeting to Richard, he seated himself beside Carrington Rexon behind the young people. Jacques Bassett stood against the closed doors at the rear. Lieutenant O'Leary unobtrusively found a place for himself.

A high, old-fashioned phonograph was wheeled out to the rink by Higgins and another servant. A box of records was carried down.

Vance, on skates, in immaculate evening attire, with a white muffler at his throat, appeared on the rink. Additional lights were turned on as he came forward.

"Ladies and gentlemen," he began in mock ceremonious style. His voice was clear and resonant. "I have been honored with the privilege of conducting this memorable event. I confidently promise you an evening of most unusual regalement."

General applause greeted his statement.

"We have with us tonight," he proceeded with exaggerated formality, "performers of wide renown. I might even say, of worldwide renown. Most of you, I am sure, will recognize each name as it is announced..."

Another round of applause drowned out his next words.

"The first of our guest stars," he resumed, "is Miss Sally Alexander. She will entertain you in her own incomparable manner."

Miss Alexander came up from the pavilion, a smiling urchin in colorful tatters, skating gracefully into the spotlight thrown from an upper window of the Manor. She sang a gay Parisian chansonette of dubious significance, and was rewarded with much laughter and cheering. Her next number was a monologue depicting an intoxicated celebrity attempting to thread his way through a bevy of admiring debutantes. Skates made the task none too easy. The small audience was genuinely amused, their approval long and loud.

Vance assisted the young woman back to the pavilion and returned with Dahlia Dunham and Chuck Throme, both in trunks and jerseys. They skated into the spotlight and made a deep bow. Vance raised the young woman's hand.

"On my right, wearing red trunks," he announced, "is Miss Dahlia Dunham—a most charmin' battler, with many a vict'ry to her credit. On my left, in white trunks, is Jockey Throme, with a list of wins quite as impressive. The two will now go through three rounds for the skate-weight championship."

The gloves were put on, the seconds waved away; the referee came forward, and the bout started. The two contenders sparred lightly for a few seconds. They went into a clinch and were separated by the referee. The slippery ice under their skates sent many of the punches far afield. Those that connected did little damage. When Vance blew his whistle at the end of the third round Miss Dunham was declared the winner by popular acclaim. Chuck Throme, taking his defeat gallantly, essayed another bow. As on an earlier occasion, he carried the obeisance too far. His skates slid out from under him. He lay prone on the ice. Vance and Miss Dunham assisted him to his feet and helped him from the rink.

Joan Rexon sat up and looked about. "I wish Ella would come," I heard her say. "She's missing all the fun. Have you seen her, Dick?"

Richard Rexon shook his head glumly. "Maybe she's outside somewhere." He went to investigate.

Next Miss Maddox and Pat McOrsay presented a skit with a homemade miniature plane on runners. This was followed by Vance's announcement of Miss Naesmith's number with Stanley Sydes. In Spanish costume they creditably performed a series of dances to the accompaniment of the records Vance placed on the phonograph. The other performers joined them for the final tango. Richard Rexon had returned to the disconsolate Joan.

"And now," came Vance's voice again, "we have a surprise for you. I can't give you the name of this performer because she is practically unknown. We call her the Masked Marvel... But one moment! I must whisper in our maestro's ear what melody he is to play." He pantomimed comically to the phonograph as he put on a new record. The lovely strains of *Geschichten aus dem Wiener Wald* came floating over the still night. And then…

A petite figure came tripping out on the ice with unbelievable ease and rhythm. Her costume of velvet and sequins shimmered gaily in the lights. A silk mask covered most of her face. Her spaced routine was exquisitely performed. With incredible grace she combined the most difficult school figures with spirals, spins, and jumps of daring originality.

Everyone gasped with delight. There was a remark that it must be Linda Höffler, the newest skating sensation. Some of the guests questioned Miss Joan and young Rexon. They disclaimed all knowledge. Carrington Rexon, when asked what famous importation he had bagged for the event, would give no information.

Each time the girl left the rink the applause was so loud and continuous that Vance had to bring her back.

Finally one voice called out, "Remove the mask!" The cry was taken up in unison. Vance whispered to the girl at his side. She permitted him to take the mask from her face. Smiling happily, Ella Gunthar stood before us.

Joan Rexon arose in triumphant delight. "I knew it was Ella!" She was almost in tears. "I always knew Ella could do it. Isn't she marvelous, Richard?"

But young Rexon was already on the terrace steps, making his way to the rink. Carrington Rexon and the doctor stepped to Miss Joan's side.

"Oh, Dad!" the girl exclaimed. "Why didn't you tell me?"

"It's as much a surprise to me as it is to you, my dear. Mr. Vance told me merely he had arranged something for you. I had no idea it was a surprise like this."

"All right, now. All right," Quayne put in admonishingly. "I think that's enough for this evening, Joan." The two men helped the girl indoors.

A noisy circle surrounded Ella Gunthar on the rink. The workmen, having been permitted to witness the performance, now moved off. The guests withdrew indoors.

Later they gathered in the drawing room. The performers came up from the pavilion, still in their costumes. Vance, showered with congratulations, disclaimed all credit.

"It's all Miss Naesmith's doing, I assure you," he told everyone.

Ella Gunthar came in, escorted by Richard Rexon. She was enthusiastically greeted on all sides. She seemed upset and nervous and remained only long enough to embrace Miss Joan and say a few words to her. Young Rexon's and Vance's offers to see her home were refused with polite determination. She hurried away alone.

The phonograph was brought back from the rink. Someone wound it up and started a record. Soon dancing began. Quayne brought the housekeeper in and directed her to get Miss Joan off to bed. The woman had a new look of pride about her and was almost cheerful as she took charge of the girl and led her from the room.

The gaiety of the party increased. Only Jacques Bassett sat morosely by himself. Quayne was about to approach him, but was buttonholed by Miss Naesmith with a request for the best antidote to seasickness. Richard Rexon joined Bassett at his table.

Vance had had enough. He bade his host good night. O'Leary came up with a questioning look. But Vance put him off.

"Let's sleep on it, Lieutenant," he said. "Come round before noon… Jolly party, what!… Cheeri-o."

O'Leary watched sullenly as Vance mounted the stairs.

# CHAPTER TWELVE

## *Queen Istar's Necklace*
*(Sunday, January 19; 9:30 a.m.)*

VANCE ROSE EARLY again Sunday. After strong coffee he invited me to stroll with him in the clear winter sunshine. Snow had fallen in the early hours of the morning; the world about us was covered with a fresh white blanket. We took a footpath that led down to the small pond in the Green Glen where we had first come upon Ella Gunthar. As we skirted a high bush at one end of the pond a small cabin came into view.

"The Green Hermit's cottage, I'll warrant," commented Vance. "Sabbath morn visit to the druid in order."

The door was slightly ajar. Vance rapped. There was no response. He pushed the door wide open. At a small table near a window sat Old Jed. He looked up without surprise.

"Good morning," Vance said pleasantly from the threshold. "May we come in?"

The old man nodded indifferently. His attention was focused on some object between his fingers. As we approached him he raised his hands. The sun fell full on a dazzling necklace of emeralds.

"Six cabochons on a chain of smaller stones," said Vance half to himself. Then admiringly to the old man: "Lovely, isn't it?"

Old Jed smiled with childish delight as he let the green stones slide between his fingers.

Vance sat down beside him. "What else have you?"

Old Jed shook his head.

"What did you do with the others?"

"No others. Only this." He spread the necklace on the table, inviting Vance to share his ecstasy. "Like the green meadows in springtime," he said mystically. "Like running streams of water—like God's trees in summer:—green, all beauty in nature is green." His eyes shone fanatically.

"Yes," said Vance, falling in with his mood. "Spring…the green of nature all about:

'And all the meadows, wide unrolled,
Were green and silver, green and gold.' "

He looked up kindly.

"Find it, Jed?"

A shake of the head from the old man.

"Where did you get it?"

Another shake of the head. "You're a friend of Miss Ella?" the hermit asked as if eager to change the subject.

"Yes. Of course. And you are too."

The grey head bobbed enthusiastically up and down. "But that fellow Mr. Richard brought home with him. Are you a friend of his?"

"Mr. Bassett? No. No friend of his. Far from it… What about him?"

"No good," declared Old Jed with strict economy of words.

Vance raised his brows slightly. "Did he give you that green necklace?"

"No!" The old man was petulant. "He came here to make trouble for Miss Ella."

"Really, now! When was that?"

"He came here last night. Before the swell doin's up at the big house. He thought Miss Ella was alone. But I saw him." Old Jed cackled. "Now he won't come here no more."

"No? Why not?"

"He won't come no more," repeated the other vaguely... "But up at the big house, Mister: you'll take care of Ella?"

"Certainly," promised Vance. "She'll be all right... But tell me, Jed; how did you get that trinket?"

The old man looked back at him in blank silence.

Vance tried strategy. "It's for Miss Ella's sake I must know."

"Miss Ella, she doesn't do anything bad."

"Then tell me where you got that necklace," persisted Vance.

The old man looked about him in perplexity. His eyes came to rest on the small phonograph we had seen Ella Gunthar using. He looked up at Vance triumphantly. "There!" He pointed to the instrument.

Vance rose and brought it to the table. He opened it up and shook it, but without disclosing anything untoward. The old man picked up the necklace, placed it on the green felt base.

"So," he said simply. "It was hidden there when I found it."

Just then the door was pushed wide open again. Ella Gunthar stood there, a smile fading from her lips as she saw us. Old Jed stood up to greet her. Vance stepped across the room, took the girl gently by the hand, and led her to the table. Her glance fell on the open phonograph with the string of gems sparkling inside. Abruptly she turned away, her face white.

"How much do you know about this, Miss Gunthar?" Vance asked indulgently.

"I don't know—anything about it." Her answer was low and hesitant.

"But you've seen it before?"

"I—think so. In the Gem Room."

"How did it happen to be hidden in your little music box? Jed says he found it there."

"I—I don't know. Maybe it's not real."

"Oh, it's real enough, my dear."

"I don't know anything about it," she repeated stubbornly.

"Now I think you're fibbing again. Do you know that just such a necklace, and many other costly stones, are missing from the Gem Room?"

She nodded. "Richard told me last night."

"Did Richard give you this?"

"No!" She glared at Vance indignantly. "And Jed doesn't know anything about it either. And neither does my father! Oh, you're all trying to pin lies on father—don't you think I know why that police officer from Winewood is always hanging around the estate?" Her words came in a passionate rush.

Vance watched the unhappy girl appraisingly. "Who, then, my dear, do you think took the emeralds?" he asked calmly.

"Who?—who?" she echoed. She bit her lips. She thought for several moments. Then, as if on sudden impulse, she blurted defiantly: "*I* took them—*I* took them, of course!"

"*You* took them!"" Vance repeated skeptically. "What else did you take besides the Istar necklace, Miss Ella?"

"I don't know just what—some loose stones."

"How did you get into the Gem Room?"

"I found the door unlocked."

"Oh, come now, Miss Ella. Mr. Rexon's not in the habit of leaving the Gem Room door unlocked."

"I found it unlocked," she insisted.

"And once inside the room, what did you do?"

"I opened two of the cases."

Vance laughed softly. "You found those unlocked too?"

She drew up with a start. Tears formed in her eyes.

"Then I—I—broke them," she stammered.

"I see, Miss Ella. Then you won't mind coming with me to the Manor to tell Mr. Rexon all about it?"

"No." She swallowed hard. "I won't mind."

Old Jed looked from Vance to the girl and back to Vance. He furrowed his brow in an attempt to concentrate.

"Mr. Vance," the girl asked timidly, "will Miss Joan have to know about it? And—and—Richard?"

"I'm afraid so," said Vance. "But perhaps not at once, my dear. Are you ready to go?"

Vance pocketed the necklace and accompanied the girl from the cabin. Again he took the footpath by which we had come. He made no further mention of the missing gems. Instead he asked: "Bassett been making himself objectionable again?"

She kept her eyes straight ahead. "It was nothing... Did Jed tell you?... I never saw Jed so angry. I think Mr. Bassett was really frightened."

The rest of the walk was in silence.

Carrington Rexon was alone in the den. Ella Gunthar entered the room as Vance held the door for her. She stepped to one side and stood shyly with her back against the wall. Vance indicated a chair. The girl looked from him to Rexon and came forward.

"Now, my dear," prompted Vance as she sat down.

She lowered her eyes, gripped the sides of the chair.

"Mr. Rexon, I—" She raised her head and then spoke very quickly. "I took the emeralds."

"You *what?*" Rexon asked in astonishment.

"I took the emeralds," she repeated more slowly.

Rexon laughed bitterly in spite of himself.

"I can prove it!" she declared recklessly. She extended her hand to Vance for the necklace. He brought it out, gave it to her. She placed it diffidently on the desk beside her.

Rexon took it up eagerly, looked at it carefully. "The Istar necklace! Ah!" Then shrewdly: "Where are the rest?"

The girl shook her head. "I won't tell you. I won't!" Her compressed lips indicated unmistakably that she would say no more.

Rexon leaned back in his chair and studied the girl critically. Then crisply: "And you're the girl my son wants to marry!"

Ella Gunthar's face suddenly flushed. Rexon's words had startled her.

"Oh, yes, my dear young lady," Rexon continued coldly. "You didn't think I knew of the affair that's been going on between you and Richard. Miss Naesmith told me about it only last night—Miss Naesmith, the girl I hoped would be his wife… Bah! After all I've done for you! You're not content to steal the love of my only son. You must take my emeralds too." He half rose in his anger. "I'm almost glad this thing has happened. It will be well worth the loss of the emeralds if I can save Richard…"

Vance stepped swiftly round the desk and put his hand on the older man's shoulder. "My dear old friend, please! Don't turn a disappointment into a tragedy."

Rexon relaxed under the persuasive pressure of Vance's hand.

Tears flooded Ella Gunthar's eyes. Vance came to her side.

"Poor child," he said soothingly, "don't you think this tragic farce has gone far enough? It's time for the truth now—all the truth you know. We're in the dark. We want your help. Some terrible forces are at work in the Manor here. Some dangerous criminal perhaps. You can help those you love only by telling us the truth. Will you?"

She took a deep breath, dried her eyes. "Yes, I will," she said with unexpected determination.

Vance sat down beside her. "Then tell me first: Whom are you trying to shield with this foolish tale of theft?"

"I—I don't know exactly. But it seemed that everyone I love had suddenly been caught in an awful trap. Poor Jed, whom you caught with the necklace; my father, whom I knew that police officer suspected of all sorts of things; and, somehow, Richard… And it was all mixed up in some horrible way with that night on the cliff when poor Lief was killed. I—I—it was all confusion. And it seemed that only I could help."

She buried her face in her hands, but when she looked up again her eyes were still dry.

"And I had to try to help them without knowing how to go about it; for I *really* didn't know… Only little things, here and there, that didn't seem to fit together."

"You poor child," murmured Vance again. "But please tell us what you do know—all the little things—anything that may come to your mind. Maybe it will help us all—especially those you love most."

"Oh, I'll try! I'll try!" She spoke eagerly and braced herself. "Perhaps you think, Mr. Vance, that I insisted on going to the inquest Friday merely as an overcurious child."

"No," returned Vance. "Naturally, I've pondered the point. But no opinion."

"Well, anyway, you know all that I heard there. I think that jury was just anxious to get a bad job off their hands." (I could see that Vance was amazed at the sagacity indicated by her remark.) "And I've heard other things, too, Mr. Vance. I've heard the workmen saying it's strange that my father should have been the one to find Lief Wallen's body… Guy Darrup is still saying I should have married Lief. Can a girl help it if she doesn't love a man? Then I've heard my father say it's strange that Jed should have known just which way to go that morning. Jed, who wouldn't harm a fly!… I've heard that my father wasn't home at midnight on the night Lief died, and that it made things look pretty dark for him… Well, *I* wasn't at home at midnight either! Does that mean *I* killed Lief Wallen?…"

She broke off.

"I'm sorry if I sound all mixed up," she resumed. "But it's because I feel all mixed up… A little before twelve that night I came here. Richard asked me to. We hadn't had a chance to speak alone together all day. We were to meet at a favorite tree we have up behind the pavilion. I waited and waited. But Richard didn't come. And then I heard him talking to somebody. He was angry, I think. But he must have gone back inside. That's when I went running down past the pavilion crying. Just as Guy Darrup said I did. But he didn't know the reason."

She paused and looked at Vance, then at Rexon.

"Anything more?" Vance gave her a searching glance.

"Haven't I said enough?" Her voice sounded weary.

"You haven't told us where you got the necklace."

"Must I?"

"It might help to clear up a deucedly involved situation, don't y' know."

"All right. But my father didn't take it!" She looked defiantly at Rexon. "I found it lying on the floor near the window in the dressing room reserved for me at the pavilion last night. I was going to return it to Mr. Rexon. But then Richard told me what had happened. I was afraid I'd be asked questions. I knew father was in the pavilion yesterday. Jed brought my costume up there for me. Father locked the room—to keep the surprise—and gave me the key. I was afraid to do anything with the necklace until I had time to think what would be best. And that's why I took it to Jed's cabin and hid it in my little music box... But my father didn't take it! And Old Jed didn't take it either!..."

Carrington Rexon looked profoundly disturbed and perplexed. Vance placed his hands on Ella Gunthar's shoulders and was about to raise her from the chair.

A knock on the door was followed by Higgins ushering in Lieutenant O'Leary with a plain-clothes man in his wake.

# CHAPTER THIRTEEN

## *The Second Murder*

*(Sunday, January 19; 11 a.m.)*

O'LEARY LOOKED FROM Vance to the girl in the chair and then at the necklace spread on the desk before Rexon.

"Where did that come from, sir?" he inquired bluntly.

Vance briefly repeated the girl's account of the finding of the necklace.

"A likely story." O'Leary's tone was sarcastic...

The telephone rang. Rexon answered. Then: "It's from New York, Vance—for you. Private line, this. Perfectly safe. Go ahead." He pushed the instrument across the desk.

O'Leary drew his officer aside and spoke earnestly to him while Vance was at the telephone.

"...What caused the delay, Sergeant?" Vance was saying. "Ah, records in Washington... I see... I'll take it word for word..." He reached for paper and pencil. He wrote out a dictated message. I recognized the excitement under his calm demeanor as he worked quickly. "Thorough as always, Sergeant." He spoke with satisfaction as he threw down the pencil. "That gives me just what I need... No. Not necess'ry for you to come. Many thanks..."

He pushed the phone back and stood up. He sighed. He folded the message he had written out, and placed it in his pocket. He sat down again and lighted a *Régie*. "Well, Lieutenant?"

O'Leary came back to Ella Gunthar's chair. "I've kept my promise to you, sir." He was calm, unofficious. "I've waited, as you asked me to. Now I have no choice but to arrest this girl and her father. I think you will agree, sir. I brought this man for the purpose." He hesitated. "Unless you have additional information that will alter my decision."

"I think I have, Lieutenant." Vance turned to the girl in the chair. "Would you join Miss Joan on the veranda, Miss Ella?"

"I'm sorry, sir." O'Leary held up his hand peremptorily. "I don't believe I can allow that."

"Oh, I say! Then send your man with her. Perfectly safe, Lieutenant."

O'Leary scowled, but complied. The girl walked slowly from the room, followed by the husky Winewood constable.

"Thanks no end." Vance tossed his cigarette into the grate. "Lieutenant, I promised you additional information. Here it is." He brought forth the folded paper from his pocket, and passed it to O'Leary.

The Lieutenant unfolded it, glanced at it with quickly moving eyes, then read it aloud: "Whisky glass submitted shows clear prints of Jasper Biset. Description also corresponds. Biset reputed head of international organization of high-pressure jewel thieves. Generally keeps in background. No cause for criminal action against him available. Better known abroad, but would be recognized here. Last tabbed in Saint Moritz, Switzerland."

O'Leary looked up blankly.

"Let me explain further." Vance spoke. "On my first evening here I saw a face. Strangely familiar. Vague association. With Amsterdam. There were eyebrows meeting above the nose. Like a black shaft. But the face wasn't right. No.

Something missin'. Should have been a mustache. Bristly. However... Mustaches come and go. On impulse, I took the glass from which the gentleman had been imbibing too much Bourbon. Sent it, with note and general description, to New York police. Hopin'... That's the verbatim report. Just received."

"Who is Jasper Biset?" O'Leary's voice was tinged with exasperation.

"Gent known to police as Jasper Biset is here under preferable name of Jacques Bassett. Guest of the Manor. More specifically of Mr. Richard Rexon."

Carrington Rexon gave a start but said nothing.

"Then you think he's the one—" began O'Leary.

"Don't know, Lieutenant. Those are all the facts I have. Bein' honest. Keepin' an open mind. Like yourself. But a chat with Biset-Bassett is clearly indicated—eh, what? Shall we do it here?"

O'Leary, somewhat dazed and uncertain, nodded.

Vance turned to Rexon. "Will you have the gentleman summoned, sir?"

Rexon, frowning deeply, rang. Higgins appeared and was given instructions. Vance paced up and down the room. He lighted a fresh *Régie*. The Lieutenant stood stoically at the window. He fumbled with his pipe.

Higgins returned. "Sorry, sir. Mr. Bassett is not in his room."

"Well, can't you find him, man?" Rexon showed impatience.

"It would seem, sir, the gentleman hasn't been in his room all night."

"Oh, my word!" Vance stood perfectly still, his cigarette halfway to his lips. "Are you sure, Higgins?"

"I knocked on the door, sir. No one answered. The door was unlocked, and I looked in, sir. The bed hasn't been slept in all night. I checked with the chambermaid, sir."

A groan escaped from Rexon.

O'Leary stood up, aggressively indignant. "I felt we should have acted sooner, Mr. Vance."

Vance ignored the implied reprimand. "Higgins, call the garage."

The butler dialed three numbers, handed the instrument to Vance.

"Any car been taken out this morning?" Vance waited a moment. "And last night?"... He put the telephone down. "Every car cozily in its place. Curious. Suppose we toddle up to the gentleman's boudoir."

The room showed no sign of disorder. One closet held a number of suits neatly arranged on their hangers. The other disclosed a grey topcoat, a tan one, two or three robes, and several pairs of shoes. Three hats rested on an upper shelf. From the closets Vance went to the bureau, inspected the drawers. These were neatly filled with the customary accessories of a man of taste. A trunk stood in one corner of the room with a matching bag beside it. Vance opened these, found them empty.

"Can't see that we'll learn anything here." He took in every detail of the room. "Suggest we go down to Winewood. Confab with the station master might prove illuminatin'."

The Lieutenant's small car was parked outside the veranda. O'Leary turned toward it as we came down the steps.

"Oh, I say!" Vance checked him. "Please! Mind functions more efficiently at lesser speed. Let's go on foot. If you don't mind."

O'Leary shrugged. We continued to the end of the pathway, swung into the vehicle road leading through the estate to the county highway. The fresh layer of snow was unmarred but for a single set of tire tracks marking the Lieutenant's arrival an hour or two earlier.

Vance lighted a cigarette. We trudged along.

"Not every day one has the opportunity to lay his hands on a murderer." O'Leary spoke glumly. "Too bad if he's got away."

"Oh, yes. Quite. Very sad. But I'm not convinced the man *is* a murderer. My own observations contraindicative. No. Not the type that deals in murder. Too suave. Wouldn't bloody his hands."

"Then you don't think he killed Wallen in an earlier attempt to get at the emeralds?" O'Leary seemed surprised.

"No—oh, no. As I said. Not the type. However..."

"But you admit he's gone off now with the gems?"

"My dear Lieutenant! I admit nothing. Just lookin' round at present. Strivin' to learn."

"That throws us back on Eric Gunthar. Has he been asked to account for himself during yesterday's incident?"

"No. Not yet. Good thought, however. I'll speak with him later. 'Where were you on the night of—?' And all that sort of thing. Might help. Might not..." Vance flung the end of his cigarette aside.

We had just passed through the large gates and taken perhaps a hundred paces on the highway toward Winewood.

O'Leary brought out his pipe. "The car would have been quicker—"

"Quicker. Yes." Vance stopped abruptly. "But not as productive of results... Look yonder, Lieutenant."

He directed our gaze into a clump of trees at one side of the roadway, just beneath the towering wall of the Rexon estate. An irregular mound of snow, with patches of black here and there, ended in a pair of patent leather shoes.

"Might have driven right past that, don't y' know." Vance stepped through the undergrowth. O'Leary followed in abashed silence.

As we came nearer, the mass resolved itself into the outlines of a hunched human form, one arm twisted crazily under the torso, the other extended straight from the shoulder.

"That, I opine, is our missing jewel expert." Vance spoke solemnly. He approached the figure, turned the face upward.

It was Jacques Bassett, in the evening attire in which I had last seen him the previous night. Now he wore a black Chesterfield as well. Vance bent down, examined the body more closely. A streak of sticky, darkened snow above the right ear caught his attention.

"Same like Wallen, Lieutenant. Not a nice business. Not at all a nice business. No."

"You're right, sir. Too much like Wallen. Same kind of wound. I don't like it either, sir... Been dead long, would you say?" O'Leary asked as Vance rose.

"Eight or ten hours. But, my word, Lieutenant! I'm not the Medical Examiner. Should have Quayne here. Shall I stagger back to the Manor and phone your Æsculapius, or would you prefer to do the chore while I wait here?"

"No need for you to stay here, sir." O'Leary was respectful. "I'll remain. If you'll be good enough to phone Doctor Quayne."

"Gladly, Lieutenant... By the by..." Vance hesitated. "Could you tell me if the emeralds are in the gentleman's attire?"

"Really shouldn't do it, sir. Against regulations." O'Leary knelt down as he spoke and made a swift examination of Bassett's pockets. He rose. "No emeralds, sir. Just the usual." Then he added quickly, "You see what this means, sir?"

Vance looked at the other from the corner of his eye. "You're far too clever for this bailiwick, Lieutenant."

"I like it here... It does throw the case back on Eric Gunthar harder than ever—doesn't it, sir?"

Vance nodded. "I'm afraid it does—theoretically. But surely, Lieutenant, you don't believe—"

"I'm not paid to believe things, sir. I'm paid to follow facts." O'Leary drew on his pipe. "And I'm afraid I'll have to go through with the arrest of Gunthar and his daughter. I'm telling you now, sir. I want to be fair."

"I understand, Lieutenant." Turning away, Vance retraced his steps to the Manor.

On the veranda a few of the guests were talking animatedly. Joan Rexon had gone indoors. Ella Gunthar sat apart from the others, looking listlessly toward the rink. She was still guarded rather ludicrously by the Winewood constable. Vance approached her.

"Listen carefully, my dear. There's real danger for you and your father. I need your help. You and I must work together.

We'll get rid of the nightmare. Here's what I want you to do. Get your skates and skating costume. Tell your father Mr. Rexon would like to see him in his den. And Old Jed too, if you can find him. This gentleman will accompany you." Vance indicated the constable. "Then you are to come back here to the rink and skate as if everything you ever wanted depended on it. Keep all the guests interested. Keep them away from the house at any cost. Skate until I give you the signal to stop. In the meantime, I'll be working hard for you and your father. Understand?"

The girl's lips quivered. Then she raised her chin and looked Vance straight in the eye. "I'll do everything you ask." There was determination, submission, heroism, in her voice. She turned toward the pavilion, the burly officer close behind her.

Vance started for the den. Carlotta Naesmith ran up inquisitively, as if to ask a question.

Vance held up his hand. "Not now, please. I have an urgent favor to ask of you. All the guests must be kept out here. Away from the house. Ella Gunthar is going to skate for them. You've hurt her much. She's suffering now. Be kind."

Before Miss Naesmith could answer, Vance continued to the den.

He found Carrington Rexon still alone there and briefly told him of the new developments.

The man sank dejectedly into a chair. "Another death!" he groaned miserably. "And the emeralds?"

"Not on him. May still be recovered."

Vance reached for the telephone. He called Quayne, apprised him of the situation, and informed him just where he would find Lieutenant O'Leary waiting by Bassett's body.

"What do you make of it all, Vance?" asked Rexon as the other sat down opposite.

"Nothing yet, old friend. Tryin' to add things up. Must make a simple sum eventually… Would you ask your housekeeper to come here, please? A few queries I'd like to put to her."

Rexon telephoned the request.

Vance rose with suppressed nervousness and went to the window. He lighted a cigarette. At length he turned and faced his host.

"I've a feeling that somewhere this morning I've missed something. Of no importance. Bothers me no end, though. Something unconsciously waited for. Hasn't happened..."

# CHAPTER FOURTEEN

## *Skating for Time*

*(Sunday, January 19; 1:15 p.m.)*

MARCIA BRUCE CAME in, dignified and composed. Vance drew up a chair for her.

"We have a few questions to put to you, Miss Bruce," he began tentatively.

"Nothing here surprises me any more," the housekeeper returned philosophically. "I'll do my best to answer."

"You know, of course, that several of the emeralds have been stolen from the Gem Room?"

"Mr. Rexon has informed me of it. That surprises me less than anything else. I'll be glad to be free of the atmosphere surrounding those stones."

"What do you mean, Bruce?" interposed Rexon.

"I might as well tell you, sir. You'll have to know sooner or later. I'm resigning immediately, sir. And leaving here for good in about a week—maybe sooner."

"Resigning! Leaving! But why, Bruce?"

The woman blushed. "Doctor Quayne has done me the honor of asking me to marry him."

Vance smiled pleasantly. "Well, well! That would have been last evening—eh, what, Miss Bruce? Just before you came for Miss Joan."

The woman seemed startled. "How could you know that?"

"Lovelight in a woman's eyes. I saw the signs. May I be the first to congratulate you."

"And I, too, am delighted to hear it, Bruce..." Rexon's voice trailed off. Then, "But couldn't you stay on? Joan would miss you..."

"And I'll be sorry to leave Miss Joan, sir. But Loomis—that is, the doctor—wants to leave Winewood. He finds it increasingly difficult to manage here—what with two younger men making such inroads on his practice."

"Where does he plan to go?"

"I'm not quite sure yet, sir. He mentioned the possibility of going abroad."

Rexon nodded resignedly. "I understand. I understand. I imagine it *is* getting a hard row for Quayne to hoe. But, Gad! I'll miss him. And you too, Bruce."

"To get back to less pleasant matters, Miss Bruce." Vance seated himself on the arm of a chair. "You must have been down on the lower floor here yesterday about noon."

"I was. I was down most of the morning, seeing about meals, and—"

"Did you see Eric Gunthar here?"

"I noticed him hovering outside the rear entrance. But I don't know whether he came into the house."

"Did you see Old Jed?"

"That hermit! He never comes near the house, sir."

"Well, can you remember anyone you did specifically see? Out in the hall there, or near the Gem Room?"

"So many of the guests were up and down." She hesitated a moment, as if to collect her thoughts. "Mr. Richard dashed through the hall once or twice. I think I saw his foreign-looking friend, too. And that treasure-hunting gentleman was hovering around. I don't know whether he was waiting for Miss

Naesmith, or what. And I saw Doctor Quayne, though I didn't have a chance to speak to him." She seemed avid for any excuse to mention the man's name.

"Was that when he arrived in the morning?" Vance asked.

"No. It was when he was leaving. He had stayed longer than usual and he was late. I remember the noon siren had blown a few minutes earlier—"

Vance sprang to his feet and held up his hand for silence. A far-away look came into his eyes. He paced back and forth nervously several times. Then he came to a sudden stop before Rexon's desk.

"That insignificant something," he remarked slowly, as he sank into a chair. "I think I have it. The siren. Haven't heard it today."

"It's not sounded on Sundays," Rexon told him.

"No. Of course not. But yesterday."

"What can the siren have to do with it all, Vance?"

"Everything. Needs a little thought." He brought out his case and selected a cigarette with marked deliberation. He walked to the window, stood gazing out for a moment. As he turned back, a soft knock on the door was followed by the timid entry of Eric Gunthar, twisting his hat nervously in his hands.

"You wanted to see me, Squire?" he asked, looking down at the floor.

It was Vance who answered his query. "You might as well know the worst, Gunthar. Lieutenant O'Leary is determined to arrest you and Miss Ella on what he calls suspicion. You must have noted he has a constable watching Miss Ella now... She came back with you?"

"Yes, sir. She did. She's down at the pavilion, changing her clothes. She said she was going to skate on the rink."

"Good," said Vance. "We must all go out and watch her anon."

"She asked me to tell you, sir, that she couldn't find Old Jed anywhere."

"Thank you. It doesn't matter... But to get back to what I was saying. I see no reason why you shouldn't be here too. No use trying to run away. The Lieutenant will arrive any minute. You're to sit there. Trust to me. Just as Ella is doing. I'll do my best. May fail. But can't be helped. Sit tight and wait. Understand?"

Nodding dejectedly, the man moved with awkward steps to the chair Vance had indicated. He continued the twirling motion of the hat in his hands for a moment. Then he placed the hat behind him and rested his head docilely on the palms of his hands. He was abashed, frightened.

Vance had scarcely resumed his own seat before Rexon's desk when another tap on the door announced the arrival of the Lieutenant and Doctor Quayne. A faint odor of gasoline accompanied them.

"I see your chariot has had another intramuscular injection, doctor," Vance said pleasantly. Quayne merely nodded.

"Greetings and congratulations, doctor," said Rexon. "Bruce has just told us of the betrothal..."

Quayne smiled and looked admiringly at Marcia Bruce. He seated himself on the long leather divan, and Miss Bruce rose from her chair and joined him.

"I felt somehow you'd be pleased, Rexon," Quayne said with some show of pride.

"Naturally. But I'll miss you both. So will Joan."

O'Leary mumbled felicitations, his gaze on the downcast figure of Gunthar perched uneasily on the edge of his chair. Then he furrowed his brow in a puzzled frown and sought Vance's eyes.

"Yes. Quite, Lieutenant. Doing the big-hearted. Knew you'd be poppin' in anon. Thought I'd have Gunthar handy for you. Trying to do my share. Always appreciative of favors."

"And the girl?"

"Waiting for you, too. After a manner of speaking. If she isn't already out on the rink she'll be there in a minute or two. Skating for the guests. Under the eagle eye of your doughty constable, of course."

O'Leary suddenly stepped back, narrowed his eyes and looked at Vance shrewdly. "What's the meaning of all this, sir? There's something underneath."

Vance smiled wearily and nodded. "Right you are, Lieutenant! Something underneath. But what? I think it's the siren—the Rexon noonday siren, Lieutenant, which echoes through the hills and—"

O'Leary broke in impatiently. "Just where is this leading, sir?"

"To a mere bit of chatting. Puttin' things together. Askin' a few questions. Searchin' our souls. Good for the soul now and then. When all that's done, you may lead Gunthar and his daughter forth. If that should still be your desire, Lieutenant."

"Sounds like hocus-pocus to me, sir."

"More or less true of all life—eh, what?"

"How long is this to take, sir?" O'Leary's restlessness was apparent. "I've gone pretty far with you already. For my part, I'm ready to take them now..."

"You shall call the time yourself, Lieutenant."

O'Leary packed his pipe. "That's fair."

"Yes—oh, yes. Always fair. May be futile at times. But fair."

# CHAPTER FIFTEEN

## *Queries and Answers*

*(Sunday, January 19; 1:45 p.m.)*

DOCTOR QUAYNE MOVED uneasily in his place on the divan. "It's a bad business," he remarked. "A bad business. Bassett's been dead at least ten hours. We had the body removed to the morgue. Another autopsy to do. From what I've seen offhand, I can only say that he met his death very much as Wallen did. But this time there is no cliff from which he might have fallen."

"You, too, noticed the similarity of the wounds, did you, doctor?" O'Leary put in.

"It could hardly be overlooked," returned Quayne. "I've never seen such a strange coincidence. If I weren't so confused by other factors I'd be willing to state under oath that both deaths were caused in the same manner."

O'Leary compressed his lips with great satisfaction and nodded energetically. "The same thought occurred to me," he said.

"I understand, Mr. Vance," the doctor went on, "that you had an official report on the man this morning that throws a rather sinister light on the matter. From what Lieutenant O'Leary has told me, I've formed a theory that I'd like to put before you."

"Pray do," said Vance eagerly.

"It is this: Obviously Bassett came here with the sole purpose of getting his hands on at least some of Mr. Rexon's emeralds. If we assume that his first attempt was made from outside and that he was surprised in his effort by the guard, Wallen, we can conclude that he had then but one course left to him. Namely, to do away with Wallen. Let us further assume that he took this course; that he was *seen* taking it, by a friend of Wallen who was, in the circumstances, helpless to prevent the murder. This second man, you may be sure, would carry the grudge, and take his revenge at the very first opportunity. These men are a very simple folk, Mr. Vance. They believe wholeheartedly in the Mosaic law 'An eye for an eye'. They wouldn't hesitate to take matters into their own hands and mete out what they consider retributive justice."

"Very plausible theory, doctor," said Vance. "Worthy of consideration." Quayne nodded in acknowledgment of the compliment. Then Vance looked abruptly at Miss Bruce, sitting beside her fiancé. "You say you saw Mr. Sydes flittin' round down here about noontime?"

She nodded.

Vance now spoke to Rexon. "Will you send for the gentleman? And your son as well. Immediately, please. Speed, old friend. The leaves are turning. The bird is on the wing. Time is running out."

Rexon rang for the butler, relayed the request to him.

In a very few minutes a knock on the door was followed by the swaggering entrance of Stanley Sydes, with Richard Rexon close behind him. The younger man walked to the window behind his father's desk and sat down on the broad sill. Sydes remained standing, resting his arms on the back of an empty chair.

"Quite a conclave here," he commented casually. "I do hope we're not all going to pass up Miss Gunthar's performance. I've never seen anyone who can claim to be her equal on ice."

"You're not alone in that opinion, Mr. Sydes," Vance remarked. "We'll try not to detain you too long… Could you possibly recall just where you were yesterday when the noonday whistle sounded? Miss Bruce here thinks she saw you about that time, wanderin' in the lower hall."

Sydes laughed boisterously. "I can't say the lady is wrong. Probably was heading for the bar to soothe my jangled nerves."

"Hope the antidote was effective." Vance smiled. "Looking tip-top today… Irrelevantly speakin', Mr. Sydes, does your interest run only to *buried* treasure?" Vance looked at the man keenly.

"I don't think I understand you, sir. As I said once before, it's the thrill of the search that lures me on. But I don't suppose any man would turn up his nose at a treasure right under his nose—if I may make a quip."

"Did you know of Mr. Rexon's collection of emeralds?"

"Strangely enough, not until I'd been here a day or two. It was other game that brought me here. However, I might add that I was genuinely disappointed when I learned we were not to see the stones, after all."

"Do you happen to know why Mr. Rexon hasn't opened the Gem Room to his guests?"

"I'm sure I haven't the faintest idea. And I haven't been presumptuous enough to inquire."

"Admirable restraint," murmured Vance. "Deservin' of appeasement. I'll answer the unasked question for you. The fact is, a number of the Rexon emeralds have disappeared from the Gem Room—undoubtedly stolen. And one of the guests—Mr. Bassett—has been murdered."

Richard Rexon rose with a bound from his place at the window.

Sydes straightened up and drew in his breath. "Incredible!" he mumbled. "Why, I saw the man only—" He broke off.

"Yes?" prompted Vance. "When *did* you see Bassett last?"

"Now that I think of it," Sydes returned lamely, "I haven't seen him today at all… Is there anything I can do?"

"Thank you. Only to rejoin the others and help Miss Gunthar keep them entertained and out of our way."

Sydes bowed himself out with a look of concern mingled with relief.

Young Rexon was conversing in an undertone with his father. He looked bewildered as he stepped back to the window. Vance turned to him.

"How much did you know about your friend Bassett, Mr. Richard?"

The young man did not answer immediately. Vance lighted a cigarette while he waited. Finally young Rexon spoke.

"Not too much, I'm afraid. Only that he seemed a likable enough chap. And he was a pleasant traveling companion."

"Hardly sufficient recommendation," grumbled the elder Rexon bitterly. "The man was a scoundrel!"

"Did you know," Vance asked carelessly, "that during his brief stay here he was annoying Miss Ella?" Richard Rexon only shook his head. Vance continued. "Old Jed found it necess'ry to reprimand him severely. Perhaps Jed did more than that…"

Eric Gunthar jumped from his chair. "You can't say that, sir! The hermit may be a queer one, but he didn't murder nobody!" The man seemed surprised at his own outburst. He sank back to his chair.

Quayne looked across at Vance with significance. "Bearing out my earlier contention, Mr. Vance."

Vance nodded abstractedly. He found an ash tray and broke the ashes from his cigarette.

"Tell me, Gunthar: was this hermit of yours friendly with Lief Wallen?"

"The hermit ain't friendly with nobody. Except, maybe, my Ella."

"Had Wallen *any* friend on the estate who would want to avenge him if he thought there had been foul play?"

"I don't know about friends. But any man of us would do that if we had cause."

"Very interestin'. And most commendable... But I think Lieutenant O'Leary has a query or two to put to you." Vance made a broad gesture with his hand, as if turning over a witness to the opposition.

"Mr. Gunthar," the Lieutenant began, "you were at Murphy's tavern the night Wallen died?"

Gunthar thought back. "Yes, I was."

"And did you go directly to your cottage from there?"

"You might say I did, sir. I only stopped outside the house here, just to see what was doin'."

"Did you see Wallen?"

"No—I don't think so," said Gunthar hesitantly. Then he amended his statement. "Or if I did, I wouldn't have noticed specially."

"Did you come up to the Manor yesterday, Gunthar?" The Lieutenant was becoming more belligerent.

"Well, I did—and I didn't. I mean, I didn't come into the house exactly."

"What did you come for?"

"To talk with the Squire." He looked uneasily at Rexon. "You see, Mr. Richard wanted I should come up here and promise the Squire I wouldn't drink no more if he'd let me keep my job. So I come up here first thing in the morning. But the Squire wasn't down yet. Later Mr. Richard come down to me where I was busy at the pavilion an' told me to go up again. I didn't want to, but Mr. Richard he wouldn't let me off. So I come up. I had a bottle with me, an' I took another drink on my way. Just to buck me up, you know. An' when I come up to the house I stopped to make up what I would say. Then I thought the Squire wouldn't like it if he could smell the liquor on me. I was outside for a bit, changing my mind this way an' that. But I didn't come in. I went back to the pavilion. After lunch Mr. Richard come down again to ask me—"

"That's enough." O'Leary interrupted the recital impatiently.

"I think, Lieutenant," Vance interposed mildly, "the doctor's theory is more plausible. However, I have known medical men who, when they did not like a diagnosis which could not be proven all the way, would substitute a more acceptable alternative based on the same principal factors."

"A discerning observation," commented Quayne dryly.

"We start then, with the admissible assumption that the guard, having frustrated an attempt to enter the Gem Room from outside, is deliberately murdered. That there is an eye witness to this murder seems not too preposterous. We know definitely that access to the room is later effected by means of Mr. Rexon's key. We likewise know, beyond a doubt, that one Bassett, with sufficient and understandable reason to be interested in the emeralds, falls victim to a second murder."

Vance paused to light a fresh *Régie.*

"We find ourselves confronted," he resumed, "with more unknown quantities than I care to cope with in a single problem: Who witnessed that first hypothetical murder? Who managed to procure the key to the Gem Room and appropriate the emeralds? Finally, who finished Bassett, and why?"

He puffed thoughtfully on his cigarette and looked about.

"Offhand," he continued, "Bassett seems the logical choice for the second factor of the puzzle." The others nodded in agreement. "If only we had found the emeralds on him—or in his room..."

"Has a thorough search been made?" asked Carrington Rexon hopefully.

Before Vance could answer, the doctor spoke again. "My dear Rexon," he said, almost as if to a child. "The man was not so simple as to have left them carelessly about. He might have wrapped them securely in a packet and mailed them off somewhere."

"A reasonable suggestion," agreed Vance. "On the other hand, I am compellingly driven to the conclusion that Bassett could not have taken the emeralds at all."

There was a murmur of surprised dissent.

"Why not, Mr. Vance?" It was O'Leary who asked the question.

"For the simple reason, Lieutenant, that he wouldn't have had the time. Mr. Rexon has told us that he heard the beginning of the noon siren just as he was struck and lost consciousness. Is that correct, old friend?"

"Absolutely, Vance. I am positive of it."

"But," interposed the doctor, "I wasn't called till after half-past twelve. I presume that no one knew of Mr. Rexon's predicament until then."

"Quite right, doctor," Vance told him. "And yet, I persist in the opinion that Bassett could not have managed it… Habit dulls our awareness of the repetitious act or sound. How many of us are conscious of the striking of a clock unless we are waiting for it? We let time glide past us unnoticed. But let a man have a train to catch or a timed appointment to keep, and the tick of his watch acquires significance for him… Is that psychologically correct, Doctor Quayne?"

"Undoubtedly," agreed Quayne. He placed a hand on the shoulder of the woman beside him; but she seemed lost in her own thoughts.

"Very well, then… Bassett joined us on the veranda almost before the echo of the siren died away. You may have noticed him."

"Can't say that I did." The doctor coughed negligently.

"Possibly not. Aloof sort of johnnie. Remained at one end of the veranda—alone. Queer thing is that I wouldn't have noticed the siren. Hadn't noticed it on other days. Habit, as I say, dulls our senses, don't y' know. But though I was unconscious of the fact at the moment, the sound was forcibly called to my attention. By yourself, doctor. Do you recall?"

"It's quite possible. I remember I was in a hurry. I'd stayed longer than I intended."

"Exactly. But the important thing is—you couldn't know, doctor, because you left us immediately—that *Bassett remained on the veranda for the next half hour at* least... Does that establish my contention?"

Again there was a subdued murmuring among the others.

"Of necessity eliminating Bassett from that phase of our little problem play, whom can we enter in his stead?... Sydes was undoubtedly speaking the truth here."

"That may be, Mr. Vance," O'Leary conceded. "But what of Eric Gunthar? I'm about ready to call time, sir."

Gunthar squirmed in his chair. Young Rexon came forward.

"If you will permit me, sir, I think I can bear out Gunthar's statements. You can depend on it, he's told you the truth."

"Yes, Lieutenant," supplemented Vance. "Let me say this for Gunthar: He's been weak. He's been foolish. He's let his normal ego and competency run to aggressiveness. Hence his enemies. Then he began drinking too much. To bolster his confidence. Not wise. No. Result: both he and his daughter are in devilish hot water. However, I'm not believin' he's guilty. And I think you will agree with me shortly, Lieutenant. A few more short minutes, please..."

He looked at O'Leary, got a grudging nod from him. Then he faced young Rexon.

"What about yourself, Mr. Richard? Could you have taken your father's emeralds and wrapped them securely in a packet—?"

He was interrupted by a half-smothered shriek from Marcia Bruce. She suddenly rose from her place on the sofa.

"Oh, my God!" she moaned as she ran from the room.

Quayne looked after her in astonishment.

Vance's question had left us all equally stunned. Young Rexon stood white and speechless facing his accuser.

"From what I've observed and heard," Vance went on relentlessly, "and leaving the question of motive aside for the moment, you seem to have had every opportunity—"

Carrington Rexon leaped from his chair and pounded the desk with his fist.

"See here, Vance!" he thundered. "This has gone far enough! If you're going to make a farce of it, I prefer to say be damned to the emeralds, and drop the matter right now."

"Rexon's quite right," put in Quayne impressively. "Think of the scandal..."

"I am thinking of it." Vance's manner remained cool. "But it is no longer a question of just the emeralds. We have certainly one murder on our hands. Possibly two. Surely, you wouldn't say 'be damned' to that."

The elder Rexon shook his head despondently. He sank back into his chair. The son, at a gesture of dismissal from Vance, resumed his former place on the window sill.

# CHAPTER SIXTEEN

## *Final Curtain*

*(Sunday, January 19; 2:40 p.m.)*

VANCE TOOK A few paces across the room. His attention was caught by a pair of eyes peering in at the window behind Richard Rexon. It was the Green Hermit. He made no move as Vance approached the window and raised it.

"Might as well join us in here, Jed," Vance suggested casually. "You'll see much better, don't y' know. And hear. More satisfact'ry, what?" He closed the window as the old man moved away. Vance came back to a chair, crossed his knees as he sat down.

Higgins opened the door with a surprised look on his face. "It's Old Jed, sir," he mumbled awkwardly.

"Yes—oh, yes. Let him come in." It was Vance who spoke.

The white-haired old man came shuffling into the room, looking from side to side as if to find a place where he might hide. He finally chose a chair in the corner nearest Vance and sat down without a word.

"Where do we stand now?" Vance began anew. "Ah, yes. We still have to determine the identity of the persons involved in a dramatic piece of mayhem and thievery."

He rose from the chair and stood leaning against it.

"Mr. Rexon tells me, Doctor Quayne, that you are planning to leave Winewood." Vance looked at the man lazily.

The doctor seemed taken aback. "Frankly, yes," he returned. "Though I don't recall having mentioned it. At any rate, I don't see what my future plans can have to do with this matter."

"You will in a moment, doctor." Vance brought out a visiting card and a pencil. He wrote a few words hastily, toyed with the card for a moment. "Our problem is falling nicely into line," he announced, looking up. "I said Bassett could not have obtained the jewels. But he could—and probably *did*—assault Mr. Rexon and secure the key to the Gem Room... Yes. He would have had just enough time for that... This assumption assigns to him half of the second rôle. But our cast is still woefully incomplete... Permit me one more question, Doctor Quayne. Just why were you determined to let me know it was after twelve yesterday?"

"I resent the imputation, sir. I was simply in a hurry."

"As you said. In a hurry to get to the Gem Room and out again, doctor?"

Quayne made no reply. Merely smiled, as at a precocious child.

The door opened suddenly. Marcia Bruce came rushing back into the room. Her face was flushed. Her hands were tearing frenziedly at the paper wrappings of a small parcel. She shot a look of disgust at the man on the divan.

In the momentary confusion Vance passed the card in his hand to Lieutenant O'Leary. The latter stepped from the room, returning almost immediately. He moved leisurely to the divan, sat down beside Quayne.

Marcia Bruce had removed the last bit of paper and now held in her trembling hands a small, crudely sewn chamois bag, tied with a bit of dental floss. She turned fiery green eyes on Quayne.

"You charlatan! You thief!" she flung at him. "Did you think I could be so easily deceived? Did you think that because of your honeyed words you could count on me to aid you and shield you in your hour of need?... Your hour of need!" she repeated disdainfully. "Hour of shame! Hour of perfidy!"

She turned from him and held the bag out to Vance. He took it from her, tossed it lightly to the desk.

Carrington Rexon, with shaking fingers, managed to get the bag opened. He emptied its contents. The brilliant gems formed a shimmering green pattern on the blotter before him. His son was again at his side. Together they examined the stones.

"I think they are all here, Vance." The elder Rexon brought out a pocket handkerchief and placed the stones, one by one, in its folds.

On the divan Quayne sat deathly pale. He seemed to have aged years in a few minutes. O'Leary moved a little closer to him.

Vance turned to the housekeeper. "May I ask how that little pouch came into your possession, madam?"

"*He* brought it to me." She pointed scornfully. "Last night. For safekeeping. It was all wrapped up. It was to be a surprise. A surprise I was to share with him when we were married and—" She broke off abruptly.

Vance bowed to the woman. "Thank you, madam. It was the tangible proof I needed... Fortunate for Mr. Rexon the banks were already closed yesterday—eh, what, doctor?"

Quayne shrugged helplessly.

"Your theory wasn't far wrong, doctor. Now, if we assign to Doctor Quayne the rôle of obtaining the gems, as circumst'nces so irresistibly suggest, the problem is no longer a problem."

"But how in the world, Vance—" Carrington Rexon was at a loss for words.

"If the good doctor will help me elucidate further... Bassett's appearance on the veranda yesterday was your cue that he had carried out his half of the plan.—Am I right, doctor?"

Quayne gave no sign that he had heard.

"And, having established for yourself an ironclad alibi through that perilous hour of noon, you had only to enter the house, take the key from where you knew he had left it for you, and the rest was simplicity itself. Your presence anywhere on the lower floor here would excite no suspicion... But won't you tell us, doctor, what form of blackmail Bassett employed to induce you to enter this scheme with him?"

Still Quayne sat in stony silence.

"Then I must resort again to our limited cast," continued Vance. "You were most helpful a little earlier, doctor. No doubt thought you were helping yourself. You suggested an eye witness to the murder of Wallen. Now, whom could we place in that rôle more appropriately than Mr. Bassett?... Of course, it would be only guesswork. But he would seem to meet every requirement..."

There was an unexpected interruption from the Green Hermit. "You're not guessing, Mister. If you mean the night Lief Wallen died, I was there. I was there because I came to look after Miss Ella. Miss Ella oughtn't to come here so late... I saw the doctor walk a ways with Lief. And I saw your Mr. Bassett walk after them. All very quiet and peaceful. I didn't know they meant harm..."

Vance suddenly turned to O'Leary with a questioning look. The Lieutenant arose, making a jerky motion of his arm, much as a magician does when he is about to produce a surprise. Gradually dropping from his sleeve, came a heavy straight wrench, about twelve inches in length, with varied square openings at each end. He passed it to Vance.

"By Jove!" said Vance evenly. "A spanner! Usually part of the tool equipment of an automobile—eh, what, doctor?"

Quayne stiffened; his eyes bulged, fastened on the telltale wrench in Vance's hand.

"Too bad your first attempt to enter the Gem Room was not more successful, doctor." Vance looked coolly at the man on the divan. "So Bassett *was* the eye witness. He must have driven a hard bargain."

Quayne now spoke for the first time. His voice was strained and bitter. "Half of what I might get. And he ran only the minimum of risk."

"And did you take the additional precaution of leaving the necklace at the pavilion in the hope of further involving Gunthar who already seemed to be seriously under suspicion?"

The doctor spread his hands in a gesture of hopelessness.

"But in the end you felt you could not trust your partner? You deemed it safer—and more profitable—to put him out of your way permanently?"

Quayne leaned forward rigidly.

"I might as well tell you everything," he said wearily. "When I was abroad two years ago, Richard introduced me to Jacques Bassett. It was an unfortunate acquaintance for me. From the first I disliked the man, though I tried to give no indication of it. Brief as our association was, I felt his evil influence. In a weak moment I was persuaded to undertake smuggling a packet of gems into this country for him. I was fairly successful. Though I was under suspicion for some time, the federal investigation was finally dropped. When I sent the rascal his share of the transaction, I thought I had put him out of my life forever... Then Richard came home and brought Bassett with him. I was distressed to see that their friendship had continued. But I could say nothing... As I have already suggested, Bassett's trip here was motivated solely by his desire to acquire the Rexon emeralds. He lost no time in re-establishing contact with me. He made it plain to me that he was fortunate to find an unwilling ally who was necessarily under his thumb. He gave me the choice of doing as he said or being exposed in the smuggling matter. He painted rosy pictures for me if I would follow his bidding... For years I've been hoping to marry Marcia Bruce..."

He sent a look of appeal across the room to the woman. She had regained her poise and looked back at him coldly.

"But I never had sufficient income to take care of her," Quayne continued. "My practice had dwindled to a point where the Rexon fee was all I could count on. In the many years of my association here, stealing the emeralds never occurred to me. The scheme was Bassett's. But I was an easy prey to his designing chicanery... Wallen interrupted our first attempt, and it became necessary to get rid of him. I had the spanner with me and used it to fracture Wallen's skull. Then we dragged him to the cliff and threw him over. It looked as if we were safe; and I wanted to quit then. But Bassett held this second crime over my head more ominously than the first. I had no choice but to go on..."

He paused briefly, then resumed.

"You've shrewdly guessed, Mr. Vance, how Bassett obtained the key for me... Late last night I met him just outside the grounds to divide the gems. Distrusting him as I did, I took the spanner along as a precaution. There was a violent dispute. He threatened me, and I used the spanner again... The rest you know..."

Quayne rose suddenly. O'Leary did likewise, a pair of manacles in one hand. Vance made a negative gesture. The doctor looked about him with clouded eyes. One hand moved slowly from his vest pocket to his mouth...

He was immediately catapulted back to the divan, in horrible convulsions. In a few seconds he was still.

"Odor of bitter almonds," Vance commented calmly. "Cyanide... Wiser than I thought. Leaves us without any problem. Eliminates the second actor in the dual performance."

A hush fell over the room. Two or three minutes passed.

O'Leary broke the silence. "But, Mr. Vance, how did you get a line on that wrench?"

"It wasn't over difficult," drawled Vance. "There were two factors missin' in the pattern. The time element, and the lethal instrument. The first was cleared up when I realized their clever ruse built round the siren. The second dawned on me when Quayne returned with you this afternoon from viewing Bassett's body. He brought a noticeable aroma of gasoline with him. And I was reminded of an evening earlier in the week when he spoke of priming the engine of his car instead of using the starter. There are two tools with which to remove the spark plugs for this process: a socket wrench, or a spanner... You will recall the nature of the injuries on Wallen's skull and on Bassett's. A linear depressed fracture over the thin temporal bone. A crushing blow with a stout steel wrench would do the trick. I mentioned just such a weapon as a possibility on the morning Wallen was found."

Vance paused to light a cigarette.

"Ordin'rily, of course, the murderous weapon is disposed of as quickly as possible. But in this case it must of necessity be kept on hand to loosen the spark plugs. I was convinced it would be found within easy reach—on the floor of his car, perhaps... Is that correct, Lieutenant?"

O'Leary nodded admiringly. "But, Mr. Vance," he said somewhat sheepishly, "suppose you hadn't been on the veranda when that siren sounded? Quayne couldn't count on your presence at the right moment."

"Obviously not. That wouldn't have mattered. He counted on Miss Joan and Miss Ella. Served his purpose admirably. Perhaps better, in fact. And yet...I don't know. He would have insisted on bringing the point up. He considered it his irrefutable 'out,' don't y' know..."

"And how," asked Carrington Rexon, "did Bassett manage to come in here without my seeing him?"

"Didn't you say you were out of the room, old friend?" Vance drew deeply on his *Régie*. "The man was patient. He was playing for big odds..."

Carlotta Naesmith burst into the room. "The poor kid's all tired out, Sir Galahad. But she says you told her to keep on skating."

Vance quickly stepped before the limp figure of Quayne on the divan. "Thank you, Miss Naesmith. I'll tell her in a moment that it's all right now. We'll all be joining you."

"Please, Sir Galahad, let me tell her." Miss Naesmith whisked from the room before Vance could reply.

The guests left Rexon Manor the next morning. Richard Rexon, too, was to drive to New York with Vance and me later in the day. Carlotta Naesmith and Stanley Sydes were the last to take their departure. We formed a somewhat subdued group on the veranda as Higgins carried their bags out.

Miss Naesmith stopped on the terrace. "You'll mail me your new address, Dick?" she called back. "I'll be sending you picture postcards from Cocos Island. I hope you'll like that, Dick."

A smile of understanding passed between the two as Carrington Rexon knit his brows.

Sydes, still on the veranda, called out: "You mean that, Goddess?"

"Nothing else but," she replied as she ran to the car. "When do we start?"

"As soon as we can get to the yacht, darling." And Sydes went after her.

A little later Vance was in Carrington Rexon's den bidding him adieu.

"The ingratitude of our young folks," Rexon complained bitterly. "I don't know what the world is coming to."

"Really, now, it isn't that bad," Vance said sympathetically. "And wasn't it you, Squire Rexon, who said something about the human heart desiring happiness for others?"

Rexon looked up at him, and a new light came slowly into his eyes.

Richard came in. "You'll see that Higgins gets my trunks off, Dad?"

"Certainly, my boy. Take care of yourself… And—before you go, son, will you bring Ella in here to me."

Walking out with a smile on his lips, Vance left the two together.

The following essay by S.S. Van Dine, originally entitled "The Twenty Rules of Writing Detective Stories," first appeared in the September 1928 edition of *The American Magazine* and is reprinted here by kind permission of the author's estate.

# *Twenty Rules for Writing Detective Stories*

The detective story is a kind of intellectual game. It is more—it is a sporting event. And the author must play fair with the reader. He can no more resort to trickeries and deceptions and still retain his honesty than if he cheated in a bridge game. He must outwit the reader, and hold the reader's interest, through sheer ingenuity. For the writing of detective stories there are very definite laws—unwritten, perhaps, but nonetheless binding; and every respectable and self-respecting concocter of literary mysteries lives up to them.

Herewith, then, is a sort of Credo, based partly on the practice of all the great writers of detective stories, and partly on the promptings of the honest author's inner conscience. To wit:

1. The reader must have equal opportunity with the detective for solving the mystery. All clues must be plainly stated and described.

2. No wilful tricks or deceptions may be played on the reader other than those played legitimately by the criminal on the detective himself.

3. There must be no love interest in the story. To introduce amour is to clutter up a purely intellectual experience with irrelevant sentiment. The business in hand is to bring a criminal to the bar of justice, not to bring a lovelorn couple to the hymeneal altar.

4. The detective himself, or one of the official investigators, should never turn out to be the culprit. This is bald trickery, on a par with offering some one a bright penny for a five-dollar gold piece. It's false pretenses.

5. The culprit must be determined by logical deductions—not by accident or coincidence or unmotivated confession. To solve a criminal problem in this latter fashion is like sending the reader on a deliberate wild goose chase, and then telling him, after he has failed, that you had the object of his search up your sleeve all the time. Such an author is no better than a practical joker.

6. The detective novel must have a detective in it; and a detective is not a detective unless he detects. His function is to gather clues that will eventually lead to the person who did the dirty work in the first chapter; and if the detective does not reach his conclusions through an analysis of those clues, he has no more solved his problem than the schoolboy who gets his answer out of the back of the arithmetic.

7. There simply must be a corpse in a detective novel, and the deader the corpse the better. No lesser crime than murder will suffice. Three hundred pages is far too much pother for a crime other than murder. After all, the reader's trouble and expenditure of energy must be rewarded. Americans are essentially humane, and therefore a tiptop murder arouses their sense of vengeance and horror. They wish to bring the perpetrator to justice;

and when "murder most foul, as in the best it is," has been committed, the chase is on with all the righteous enthusiasm of which the thrice gentle reader is capable.

8. The problem of the crime must be solved by strictly naturalistic means. Such methods for learning the truth as slate-writing, ouija boards, mind reading, spiritualistic séances, crystal-gazing, and the like, are taboo. A reader has a chance when matching his wits with a rationalistic detective, but if he must compete with the world of spirits and go chasing about the fourth dimension of metaphysics, he is defeated *ab initio*.

9. There must be but one detective—that is, but one protagonist of deduction—one *deus ex machina*. To bring the minds of three or four, or sometimes a gang of detectives to bear on a problem is not only to disperse the interest and break the direct thread of logic, but to take an unfair advantage of the reader, who, at the outset, pits his mind against that of the detective and proceeds to do mental battle. If there is more than one detective the reader doesn't know who his co-deductor is. It's like making the reader run a race with a relay team.

10. The culprit must turn out to be a person who has played a more or less prominent part in the story—that is, a person with whom the reader is familiar and in whom he takes an interest. For a writer to fasten the crime, in the final chapter, on a stranger or person who has played a wholly unimportant part in the tale, is to confess to his inability to match wits with the reader.

11. Servants—such as butlers, footmen, valets, gamekeepers, cooks, and the like—must not be chosen by the author as the culprit. This is begging a noble question. It is a too easy solution. It is unsatisfactory, and

makes the reader feel that his time has been wasted. The culprit must be a decidedly worthwhile person—one that wouldn't ordinarily come under suspicion; for if the crime was the sordid work of a menial, the author would have had no business to embalm it in book form.

12. There must be but one culprit, no matter how many murders are committed. The culprit may, of course, have a minor helper or co-plotter, but the entire onus must rest on one pair of shoulders: the entire indignation of the reader must be permitted to concentrate on a single black nature.

13. Secret societies, camorras, mafias, *et al.*, have no place in a detective story. Here the author gets into adventure fiction and secret-service romance. A fascinating and truly beautiful murder is irremediably spoiled by any such wholesale culpability. To be sure, the murderer in a detective novel should be given a sporting chance, but it is going too far to grant him a secret society (with its ubiquitous havens, mass protection, etc.) to fall back on. No high-class, self-respecting murderer would want such odds in his jousting-bout with the police.

14. The method of murder, and the means of detecting it, must be rational and scientific. That is to say, pseudoscience and purely imaginative and speculative devices are not to be tolerated in the *roman policier*. For instance, the murder of a victim by a newly found element—a super-radium, let us say—is not a legitimate problem. Nor may a rare and unknown drug, which has its existence only in the author's imagination, be administered. A detective-story writer must limit himself, toxicologically speaking, to the pharmacopœia. Once an author soars into the realm of fantasy, in the Jules Verne

manner, he is outside the bounds of detective fiction, cavorting in the uncharted reaches of adventure.

15. The truth of the problem must at all times be apparent—provided the reader is shrewd enough to see it. By this I mean that if the reader, after learning the explanation for the crime, should reread the book, he would see that the solution had, in a sense, been staring him in the face—that all the clues really pointed to the culprit—and that, if he had been as clever as the detective, he could have solved the mystery himself without going on to the final chapter. That the clever reader does often thus solve the problem goes without saying. And one of my basic theories of detective fiction is that, if a detective story is fairly and legitimately constructed, it is impossible to keep the solution from all readers. There will inevitably be a certain number of them just as shrewd as the author; and if the author has shown the proper sportsmanship and honesty in his statement and projection of the crime and its clues, these perspicacious readers will be able, by analysis, elimination and logic, to put their finger on the culprit as soon as the detective does. And herein lies the zest of the game. Herein we have an explanation for the fact that readers who would spurn the ordinary "popular" novel will read detective stories unblushingly.

16. A detective novel should contain no long descriptive passages, no literary dallying with side issues, no subtly worked-out character analyses, no "atmospheric" preoccupations. Such matters have no vital place in a record of crime and deduction. They hold up the action, and introduce issues irrelevant to the main purpose, which is to state a problem, analyze it, and bring it to a successful conclusion. To be sure, there must be a sufficient descriptiveness and character delineation to

give the novel verisimilitude; but when an author of a detective story has reached that literary point where he has created a gripping sense of reality and enlisted the reader's interest and sympathy in the characters and the problem, he has gone as far in the purely "literary" technique as is legitimate and compatible with the needs of a criminal-problem document. A detective story is a grim business, and the reader goes to it not for literary furbelows and style and beautiful descriptions and the projection of moods, but for mental stimulation and intellectual activity—just as he goes to a ball game or to a crossword puzzle. Lectures between innings at the Polo Grounds on the beauties of nature would scarcely enhance the interest in the struggle between two contesting baseball nines; and dissertations on etymology and orthography interspersed in the definitions of a crossword puzzle would tend only to irritate the solver bent on making the words interlock correctly.

17. A professional criminal must never be shouldered with the guilt of a crime in a detective story. Crimes by housebreakers and bandits are the province of the police department—not of authors and brilliant amateur detectives. Such crimes belong to the routine work of the Homicide Bureaus. A really fascinating crime is one committed by a pillar of a church, or a spinster noted for her charities.

18. A crime in a detective story must never turn out to be an accident or a suicide. To end an odyssey of sleuthing with such an anticlimax is to play an unpardonable trick on the reader. If a book buyer should demand his two dollars back on the ground that the crime was a fake, any court with a sense of justice would decide in his favor and add a stinging reprimand to the author who thus hoodwinked a trusting and kindhearted reader.

19. The motives for all crimes in detective stories should be personal. International plottings and war politics belong in a different category of fiction—in secret-service tales, for instance. But a murder story must be kept *gemütlich*, so to speak. It must reflect the reader's everyday experiences, and give him a certain outlet for his own repressed desires and emotions.

20. And (to give my Credo an even score of items) I herewith list a few of the devices which no self-respecting detective-story writer will now avail himself of. They have been employed too often, and are familiar to all true lovers of literary crime. To use them is a confession of the author's ineptitude and lack of originality.
    (a) Determining the identity of the culprit by comparing the butt of a cigarette left at the scene of the crime with the brand smoked by a suspect.
    (b) The bogus spiritualistic séance to frighten the culprit into giving himself away.
    (c) Forged fingerprints.
    (d) The dummy-figure alibi.
    (e) The dog that does not bark and thereby reveals the fact that the intruder is familiar.
    (f) The final pinning of the crime on a twin, or a relative who looks exactly like the suspected, but innocent, person.
    (g) The hypodermic syringe and the knockout drops.
    (h) The commission of the murder in a locked room after the police have actually broken in.
    (i) The word-association test for guilt.
    (j) The cipher, or code letter, which is eventually unravelled by the sleuth.

We hope you enjoyed following Philo Vance through his final adventure in *The Winter Murder Case*. If you missed a few earlier episodes, fear not! All twelve novels in the series are available from Felony & Mayhem, wherever fine books are sold. And to whet your appetite, we're offering the opening chapters of Philo's first outing, *The Benson Murder Case*; read on to see how it all began...

# THE BENSON MURDER CASE

## CHAPTER ONE

### *Philo Vance at Home*

*(Friday, June 14; 8.30 a.m.)*

IT HAPPENED THAT, on the morning of the momentous June the fourteenth when the discovery of the murdered body of Alvin H. Benson created a sensation which, to this day, has not entirely died away, I had breakfasted with Philo Vance in his apartment. It was not unusual for me to share Vance's luncheons and dinners, but to have breakfast with him was something of an occasion. He was a late riser, and it was his habit to remain *incommunicado* until his midday meal.

The reason for this early meeting was a matter of business—or, rather, of æsthetics. On the afternoon of the previous day Vance had attended a preview of Vollard's collection of Cézanne watercolors at the Kessler Galleries, and having seen several pictures he particularly wanted, he had invited me to an early breakfast to give me instructions regarding their purchase.

A word concerning my relationship with Vance is necessary to clarify my rôle of narrator in this chronicle. The legal tradition is deeply imbedded in my family, and when my preparatory-school days were over, I was sent, almost as a matter of course, to Harvard to study law. It was there I met Vance, a reserved, cynical, and caustic freshman who was the bane of his professors and the fear of his fellow classmen. Why he should have chosen me, of all the students at the university, for his extra-scholastic association, I have never been able to understand fully. My own liking for Vance was simply explained: he fascinated and interested me, and supplied me with a novel kind of intellectual diversion. In his liking for me, however, no such basis of appeal was present. I was (and am now) a commonplace fellow, possessed of a conservative and rather conventional mind. But, at least, my mentality was not rigid, and the ponderosity of the legal procedure did not impress me greatly—which is why, no doubt, I had little taste for my inherited profession—and it is possible that these traits found certain affinities in Vance's unconscious mind. There is, to be sure, the less consoling explanation that I appealed to Vance as a kind of foil, or anchorage, and that he sensed in my nature a complementary antithesis to his own. But whatever the explanation, we were much together; and, as the years went by, that association ripened into an inseparable friendship.

Upon graduation I entered my father's law firm—Van Dine and Davis—and after five years of dull apprenticeship I was taken into the firm as the junior partner. At present I am the second Van Dine of Van Dine, Davis and Van Dine, with offices at 120 Broadway. At about the time my name first appeared on the letterheads of the firm, Vance returned from

Europe, where he had been living during my legal novitiate, and, an aunt of his having died and made him her principal beneficiary, I was called upon to discharge the technical obligations involved in putting him in possession of his inherited property.

This work was the beginning of a new and somewhat unusual relationship between us. Vance had a strong distaste for any kind of business transaction, and in time I became the custodian of all his monetary interests and his agent at large. I found that his affairs were various enough to occupy as much of my time as I cared to give to legal matters, and as Vance was able to indulge the luxury of having a personal legal factotum, so to speak, I permanently closed my desk at the office and devoted myself exclusively to his needs and whims.

If, up to the time when Vance summoned me to discuss the purchase of the Cézannes, I had harbored any secret or repressed regrets for having deprived the firm of Van Dine, Davis and Van Dine of my modest legal talents, they were permanently banished on that eventful morning; for, beginning with the notorious Benson murder, and extending over a period of nearly four years, it was my privilege to be a spectator of what I believe was the most amazing series of criminal cases that ever passed before the eyes of a young lawyer. Indeed, the grim dramas I witnessed during that period constitute one of the most astonishing secret documents in the police history of this country.

Of these dramas Vance was the central character. By an analytical and interpretative process which, as far as I know, has never before been applied to criminal activities, he succeeded in solving many of the important crimes on which both the police and the District Attorney's office had hopelessly fallen down.

Due to my peculiar relations with Vance it happened that not only did I participate in all the cases with which he was connected, but I was also present at most of the informal discussions concerning them which took place between him and the District Attorney; and, being of methodical temperament, I kept a fairly complete record of them. In addition, I noted down (as accurately as memory permitted) Vance's unique psychological methods of determining guilt, as he explained them from time to time. It is fortunate that I performed this gratuitous labor of accumulation and transcription, for now that circumstances have unexpectedly rendered possible my making the cases public, I am able to present them in full detail and with all their various sidelights and succeeding steps—a task that would be impossible were it not for my numerous clippings and *adversaria*.

Fortunately, too, the first case to draw Vance into its ramifications was that of Alvin Benson's murder. Not only did it prove one of the most famous of New York's *causes célèbres*, but it gave Vance an excellent opportunity of displaying his rare talents of deductive reasoning, and, by its nature and magnitude, aroused his interest in a branch of activity which heretofore had been alien to his temperamental promptings and habitual predilections.

The case intruded upon Vance's life suddenly and unexpectedly, although he himself had, by a casual request made to the District Attorney over a month before, been the involuntary agent of this destruction of his normal routine. The thing, in fact, burst upon us before we had quite finished our breakfast on that mid-June morning, and put an end temporarily to all business connected with the purchase of the Cézanne paintings. When, later in the day, I visited the Kessler Galleries, two of the watercolors that Vance had particularly desired had been sold; and I am convinced that, despite his success in the unravelling of the Benson murder mystery and his saving of at least one innocent person from arrest, he has never to this day felt entirely compensated for the loss of those two little sketches on which he had set his heart.

As I was ushered into the living room that morning by Currie, a rare old English servant who acted as Vance's butler, valet, major-domo and, on occasions, specialty cook, Vance was sitting in a large armchair, attired in a surah silk dressing gown and grey suède slippers, with Vollard's book on Cézanne open across his knees.

"Forgive my not rising, Van," he greeted me casually. "I have the whole weight of the modern evolution in art resting on my legs. Furthermore, this plebeian early rising fatigues me, y' know."

He riffled the pages of the volume, pausing here and there at a reproduction.

"This chap Vollard," he remarked at length, "has been rather liberal with our art-fearing country. He has sent a really goodish collection of his Cézannes here. I viewed 'em yesterday with the proper reverence and, I might add, unconcern, for Kessler was watching me; and I've marked the ones I want you to buy for me as soon as the gallery opens this morning."

He handed me a small catalogue he had been using as a bookmark.

"A beastly assignment, I know," he added, with an indolent smile. "These delicate little smudges with all their blank paper will prob'bly be meaningless to your legal mind—they're so unlike a neatly typed brief, don't y' know. And you'll no doubt think some of 'em are hung upside down—one of 'em is, in fact, and even Kessler doesn't know it. But don't fret, Van old dear. They're very beautiful and valuable little knick-knacks, and rather inexpensive when one considers what they'll be bringing in a few years. Really an excellent investment for some money-loving soul, y' know—inf'nitely better than that Lawyer's Equity Stock over which you grew so eloquent at the time of my dear Aunt Agatha's death."*

Vance's one passion (if a purely intellectual enthusiasm may be called a passion) was art—not art in its narrow, personal aspects, but in its broader, more universal significance. And art

---

* *As a matter of fact, the same watercolors that Vance obtained for $250 and $300 were bringing three times as much four years later.*

was not only his dominating interest but his chief diversion. He was something of an authority on Japanese and Chinese prints; he knew tapestries and ceramics; and once I heard him give an impromptu *causerie* to a few guests on Tanagra figurines, which, had it been transcribed, would have made a most delightful and instructive monograph.

Vance had sufficient means to indulge his instinct for collecting, and possessed a fine assortment of pictures and *objets d'art.* His collection was heterogeneous only in its superficial characteristics: every piece he owned embodied some principle of form or line that related it to all the others. One who knew art could feel the unity and consistency in all the items with which he surrounded himself, however widely separated they were in point of time or *métier* or surface appeal. Vance, I have always felt, was one of those rare human beings, a collector with a definite philosophic point of view.

His apartment in East Thirty-eighth Street—actually the two top floors of an old mansion, beautifully remodelled and in part rebuilt to secure spacious rooms and lofty ceilings—was filled, but not crowded, with rare specimens of oriental and occidental, ancient and modern, art. His paintings ranged from the Italian primitives to Cézanne and Matisse; and among his collection of original drawings were works as widely separated as those of Michelangelo and Picasso. Vance's Chinese prints constituted one of the finest private collections in this country. They included beautiful examples of the work of Ririomin, Rianchu, Jinkomin, Kakei and Mokkei.

"The Chinese," Vance once said to me, "are the truly great artists of the East. They were the men whose work expressed most intensely a broad philosophic spirit. By contrast the Japanese were superficial. It's a long step between the little more than decorative *souci* of a Hokusai and the profoundly thoughtful and conscious artistry of a Ririomin. Even when Chinese art degenerated under the Manchus, we find in it a deep philosophic quality—a spiritual *sensibilité*, so to speak. And in the modern copies of copies—what is called the *bunjinga* style—we still have pictures of profound meaning."

Vance's catholicity of taste in art was remarkable. His collection was as varied as that of a museum. It embraced a black-figured amphora by Amasis, a proto-Corinthian vase in the Ægean style, Koubatcha and Rhodian plates, Athenian pottery, a sixteenth-century Italian holy-water stoup of rock crystal, pewter of the Tudor period (several pieces bearing the double-rose hallmark), a bronze plaque by Cellini, a triptych of Limoges enamel, a Spanish retable of an altarpiece by Vallfogona, several Etruscan bronzes, an Indian Greco Buddhist, a statuette of the Goddess Kuan Yin from the Ming Dynasty, a number of very fine Renaissance woodcuts, and several specimens of Byzantine, Carolingian and early French ivory carvings.

His Egyptian treasures included a gold jug from Zakazik, a statuette of the Lady Nai (as lovely as the one in the Louvre), two beautifully carved steles of the First Theban Age, various small sculptures comprising rare representations of Hapi and Amset, and several Arrentine bowls carved with Kalathiskos dancers. On top of one of his embayed Jacobean bookcases in the library, where most of his modern paintings and drawings were hung, was a fascinating group of African sculpture—ceremonial masks and statuette-fetishes from French Guinea, the Sudan, Nigeria, the Ivory Coast, and the Congo.

A definite purpose has animated me in speaking at such length about Vance's art instinct, for, in order to understand fully the melodramatic adventures which began for him on that June morning, one must have a general idea of the man's *penchants* and inner promptings. His interest in art was an important—one might almost say the dominant—factor in his personality. I have never met a man quite like him—a man so apparently diversified, and yet so fundamentally consistent.

Vance was what many would call a dilettante. But the designation does him injustice. He was a man of unusual culture and brilliance. An aristocrat by birth and instinct, he held himself severely aloof from the common world of men. In his manner there was an indefinable contempt for inferiority of all kinds. The great majority of those with whom he came in contact regarded him as a snob. Yet there was in his condescension and disdain no trace of spuriousness. His snobbishness was intellectual as well as social. He detested stupidity even more, I believe, than he did vulgarity or bad taste. I have heard him on several occasions quote Fouché's famous line: *C'est plus qu'un crime; c'est une faute.* And he meant it literally.

Vance was frankly a cynic, but he was rarely bitter: his was a flippant, Juvenalian cynicism. Perhaps he may best be described as a bored and supercilious, but highly conscious and penetrating, spectator of life. He was keenly interested in all human reactions; but it was the interest of the scientist, not the humanitarian. Withal he was a man of rare personal charm. Even people who found it difficult to admire him found it equally difficult not to like him. His somewhat quixotic mannerisms and his slightly English accent and inflection—a heritage of his postgraduate days at Oxford—impressed those who did not know him well as affectations. But the truth is, there was very little of the *poseur* about him.

He was unusually good-looking, although his mouth was ascetic and cruel, like the mouths on some of the Medici portraits;* moreover, there was a slightly derisive hauteur in the lift of his eyebrows. Despite the aquiline severity of his lineaments, his face was highly sensitive. His forehead was full and sloping—it was the artist's, rather than the scholar's, brow. His cold grey eyes were widely spaced. His nose was straight and slender, and his chin narrow but prominent, with an unusually

---

* *I am thinking particularly of Bronzino's portraits of Pietro de' Medici and Cosimo de' Medici, in the National Gallery, and of Vasari's medallion portrait of Lorenzo de' Medici in the Vecchio Palazzo, Florence.*

deep cleft. When I saw John Barrymore recently in *Hamlet*, I was somehow reminded of Vance; and once before, in a scene of *Cæsar and Cleopatra* played by Forbes-Robertson, I received a similar impression.*

Vance was slightly under six feet, graceful, and giving the impression of sinewy strength and nervous endurance. He was an expert fencer and had been the Captain of the University's fencing team. He was mildly fond of outdoor sports and had a knack of doing things well without any extensive practice. His golf handicap was only three; and one season he had played on our championship polo team against England. Nevertheless, he had a positive antipathy to walking and would not go a hundred yards on foot if there was any possible means of riding.

In his dress he was always fashionable—scrupulously correct to the smallest detail—yet unobtrusive. He spent considerable time at his clubs: his favorite was the Stuyvesant, because, as he explained to me, its membership was drawn largely from the political and commercial ranks, and he was never drawn into a discussion which required any mental effort. He went occasionally to the more modern operas and was a regular subscriber to the symphony concerts and chamber-music recitals.

Incidentally, he was one of the most unerring poker players I have ever seen. I mention this fact not merely because it was unusual and significant that a man of Vance's type should have preferred so democratic a game to bridge or chess, for instance, but because his knowledge of the science of human psychology involved in poker had an intimate bearing on the chronicles I am about to set down.

---

* *Once when Vance was suffering from sinusitis, he had an X-ray photograph of his head made; and the accompanying chart described him as a "marked dolichocephalic" and a "disharmonious Nordic." It also contained the following data:—cephalic index 75; nose, leptorhine, with an index of 48; facial angle, 85°; vertical index, 72; upper facial index, 54; interpupilary width, 67; chin, masognathous, with an index of 103; sella turcica, abnormally large.*

Vance's knowledge of psychology was indeed uncanny. He was gifted with an instinctively accurate judgment of people, and his study and reading had coordinated and rationalized this gift to an amazing extent. He was well grounded in the academic principles of psychology, and all his courses at college had either centered about this subject or been subordinated to it. While I was confining myself to a restricted area of torts and contracts, constitutional and common law, equity, evidence, and pleading, Vance was reconnoitring the whole field of cultural endeavor. He had courses in the history of religions, the Greek classics, biology, civics, and political economy, philosophy, anthropology, literature, theoretical and experimental psychology, and ancient and modern languages.* But it was, I think, his courses under Münsterberg and William James that interested him the most.

Vance's mind was basically philosophical—that is, philosophical in the more general sense. Being singularly free from the conventional sentimentalities and current superstitions, he could look beneath the surface of human acts into actuating impulses and motives. Moreover, he was resolute both in his avoidance of any attitude that savored of credulousness, and in his adherence to cold, logical exactness in his mental processes.

"Until we can approach all human problems," he once remarked, "with the clinical aloofness and cynical contempt of a doctor examining a guinea pig strapped to a board, we have little chance of getting at the truth."

Vance led an active, but by no means animated, social life—a concession to various family ties. But he was not a social

---

* *"Culture," Vance said to me shortly after I had met him, "is polyglot; and the knowledge of many tongues is essential to an understanding of the world's intellectual and æsthetic achievements. Especially are the Greek and Latin classics vitiated by translation." I quote the remark here because his omnivorous reading in languages other than English, coupled with his amazingly retentive memory, had a tendency to affect his own speech. And while it may appear to some that his speech was at times pedantic, I have tried, throughout these chronicles, to quote him literally, in the hope of presenting a portrait of the man as he was.*

animal—I cannot remember ever having met a man with so undeveloped a gregarious instinct—and when he went forth into the social world, it was generally under compulsion. In fact, one of his "duty" affairs had occupied him on the night before that memorable June breakfast; otherwise, we would have consulted about the Cézannes the evening before; and Vance groused a good deal about it while Currie was serving our strawberries and eggs *Bénédictine*. Later on I was to give profound thanks to the God of Coincidence that the blocks had been arranged in just that pattern; for had Vance been slumbering peacefully at nine o'clock when the District Attorney called, I would probably have missed four of the most interesting and exciting years of my life; and many of New York's shrewdest and most desperate criminals might still be at large.

Vance and I had just settled back in our chairs for our second cup of coffee and a cigarette when Currie, answering an impetuous ringing of the front-door bell, ushered the District Attorney into the living room.

"By all that's holy!" he exclaimed, raising his hands in mock astonishment. "New York's leading *flâneur* and art connoisseur is up and about!"

"And I am suffused with blushes at the disgrace of it," Vance replied.

It was evident, however, that the District Attorney was not in a jovial mood. His face suddenly sobered. "Vance, a serious thing has brought me here. I'm in a great hurry, and merely dropped by to keep my promise… The fact is, Alvin Benson has been murdered."

Vance lifted his eyebrows languidly.

"Really, now," he drawled. "How messy! But he no doubt deserved it. In any event, that's no reason why you should repine. Take a chair and have a cup of Currie's incomp'rable coffee." And before the other could protest, he rose and pushed a bell-button.

Markham hesitated a second or two.

"Oh, well. A couple of minutes won't make any difference. But only a gulp." And he sank into a chair facing us.

# CHAPTER TWO

## *At the Scene of the Crime*

*(Friday, June 14; 9 a.m.)*

JOHN F.-X. MARKHAM, as you remember, had been elected District Attorney of New York County on the Independent Reform Ticket during one of the city's periodical reactions against Tammany Hall. He served his four years, and would probably have been elected to a second term had not the ticket been hopelessly split by the political juggling of his opponents. He was an indefatigable worker, and projected the District Attorney's office into all manner of criminal and civil investigations. Being utterly incorruptible, he not only aroused the fervid admiration of his constituents, but produced an almost unprecedented sense of security in those who had opposed him on partisan lines.

He had been in office only a few months when one of the newspapers referred to him as the Watch Dog; and the sobriquet clung to him until the end of his administration. Indeed, his record as a successful prosecutor during the four years of his incumbency was such a remarkable one that even today it is not infrequently referred to in legal and political discussions.

Markham was a tall, strongly built man in the middle forties, with a clean-shaven, somewhat youthful face which belied his uniformly grey hair. He was not handsome according to conventional standards, but he had an unmistakable air of distinction, and was possessed of an amount of social culture rarely found in our latter-day political office-holders. Withal he was a man of brusque and vindictive temperament; but his brusqueness was an incrustation on a solid foundation of good breeding, not—as is usually the case—the roughness of substructure showing through an inadequately superimposed crust of gentility.

When his nature was relieved of the stress of duty and care, he was the most gracious of men. But early in my acquaintance with him I had seen his attitude of cordiality suddenly displaced by one of grim authority. It was as if a new personality—hard, indomitable, symbolic of eternal justice—had in that moment been born in Markham's body. I was to witness this transformation many times before our association ended. In fact, this very morning, as he sat opposite to me in Vance's living room, there was more than a hint of it in the aggressive sternness of his expression; and I knew that he was deeply troubled over Alvin Benson's murder.

He swallowed his coffee rapidly, and was setting down the cup, when Vance, who had been watching him with quizzical amusement, remarked:

"I say, why this sad preoccupation over the passing of one Benson? You weren't, by any chance, the murderer, what?"

Markham ignored Vance's levity.

"I'm on my way to Benson's. Do you care to come along? You asked for the experience, and I dropped in to keep my promise."

I then recalled that several weeks before at the Stuyvesant Club, when the subject of the prevalent homicides in New York was being discussed, Vance had expressed a desire to accompany the District Attorney on one of his investigations; and that Markham had promised to take him on his next important case. Vance's interest in the psychology of human behaviour had prompted the desire, and his friendship with Markham, which had been of long standing, had made the request possible.

"You remember everything, don't you?" Vance replied lazily. "An admirable gift, even if an uncomfortable one." He glanced at the clock on the mantel: it lacked a few minutes of nine. "But what an indecent hour! Suppose someone should see me."

Markham moved forward impatiently in his chair.

"Well, if you think the gratification of your curiosity would compensate you for the disgrace of being seen in public at nine o'clock in the morning, you'll have to hurry. I certainly won't take you in dressing gown and bedroom slippers. And I most certainly won't wait over five minutes for you to get dressed."

"Why the haste, old dear?" Vance asked, yawning. "The chap's dead, don't y' know; he can't possibly run away."

"Come, get a move on, you orchid," the other urged. "This affair is no joke. It's damned serious, and from the looks of it, it's going to cause an ungodly scandal. What are you going to do?"

"Do? I shall humbly follow the great avenger of the common people," returned Vance, rising and making an obsequious bow.

He rang for Currie, and ordered his clothes brought to him.

"I'm attending a levee which Mr. Markham is holding over a corpse, and I want something rather spiffy. Is it warm enough for a silk suit?... And a lavender tie, by all means."

"I trust you won't also wear your green carnation," grumbled Markham.

"Tut! Tut!" Vance chided him. "You've been reading Mr. Hichens. Such heresy in a District Attorney! Anyway, you know full well I never wear *boutonnières.* The decoration has fallen into disrepute. The only remaining devotees of the practice are roués and saxophone players... But tell me about the departed Benson."

Vance was now dressing, with Currie's assistance, at a rate of speed I had rarely seen him display in such matters. Beneath his bantering pose I recognized the true eagerness of the man for a new experience and one that promised such dramatic possibilities for his alert and observing mind.

"You knew Alvin Benson casually, I believe," the District Attorney said. "Well, early this morning his housekeeper 'phoned the local precinct station that she had found him shot through the head, fully dressed and sitting in his favorite chair in his living room. The message, of course, was put through at once to the Telegraph Bureau at Headquarters, and my assistant on duty notified me immediately. I was tempted to let the case follow the regular police routine. But half an hour later Major Benson, Alvin's brother, 'phoned me and asked me, as a special favor, to take charge. I've known the Major for twenty years and I couldn't very well refuse. So I took a hurried breakfast and started for Benson's house. He lived in West Forty-eighth Street; and as I passed your corner I remembered your request and dropped by to see if you cared to go along."

"Most consid'rate," murmured Vance, adjusting his four-in-hand before a small polychrome mirror by the door. Then he turned to me. "Come, Van. We'll all gaze upon the defunct Benson. I'm sure some of Markham's sleuths will unearth the fact that I detested the bounder and accuse me of the crime; and I'll feel safer, don't y' know, with legal talent at hand... No objections—eh, what, Markham?"

"Certainly not," the other agreed readily, although I felt that he would rather not have had me along. But I was too deeply interested in the affair to offer any ceremonious objections and I followed Vance and Markham downstairs.

As we settled back in the waiting taxicab and started up Madison Avenue, I marvelled a little, as I had often done before, at the strange friendship of these two dissimilar men beside me—Markham forthright, conventional, a trifle austere, and over-serious in his dealings with life; and Vance casual, mercurial, debonair, and whimsically cynical in the face of the grimmest realities. And yet this temperamental diversity seemed, in some wise, the very cornerstone of their friendship: it was as if each saw in the other some unattainable field of experience and sensation that had been denied himself. Markham represented to Vance the solid and immutable realism of life, whereas Vance symbolized for Markham the carefree, exotic, gypsy spirit of intellectual adventure. Their intimacy, in fact, was even greater than showed on the surface; and despite Markham's exaggerated deprecations of the other's attitudes and opinions, I believe he respected Vance's intelligence more profoundly than that of any other man he knew.

As we rode uptown that morning Markham appeared preoccupied and gloomy. No word had been spoken since we left the apartment; but as we turned west into Forty-eighth Street Vance asked:

"What is the social etiquette of these early-morning murder functions, aside from removing one's hat in the presence of the body?"

"You keep your hat on," growled Markham.

"My word! Like a synagogue, what? Most int'restin'! Perhaps one takes off one's shoes so as not to confuse the footprints."

"No," Markham told him. "The guests remain fully clothed—in which the function differs from the ordinary evening affairs of your smart set."

"My *dear* Markham!"—Vance's tone was one of melancholy reproof—"The horrified moralist in your nature is at work again. That remark of yours was pos'tively Epworth Leaguish."

Markham was too abstracted to follow up Vance's badinage.

"There are one or two things," he said soberly, "that I think I'd better warn you about. From the looks of it, this case is going to cause considerable noise, and there'll be a lot of jealousy and battling for honors. I won't be fallen upon and caressed affectionately by the police for coming in at this stage of the game; so be careful not to rub their bristles the wrong way. My assistant, who's there now, tells me he thinks the Inspector has put Heath in charge. Heath's a sergeant in the Homicide Bureau, and is undoubtedly convinced at the present moment that I'm taking hold in order to get the publicity."

"Aren't you his technical superior?" asked Vance.

"Of course; and that makes the situation just so much more delicate... I wish to God the Major hadn't called me up."

"*Eheu!*" sighed Vance. "The world is full of Heaths. Beastly nuisances."

"Don't misunderstand me," Markham hastened to assure him. "Heath is a good man—in fact, as good a man as we've got. The mere fact that he was assigned to the case shows how seriously the affair is regarded at Headquarters. There'll be no unpleasantness about my taking charge, you understand; but I want the atmosphere to be as halcyon as possible. Heath'll resent my bringing along you two chaps as spectators, anyway; so I beg of you, Vance, emulate the modest violet."

"I prefer the blushing rose, if you don't mind," Vance protested. "However, I'll instantly give the hypersensitive Heath one of my choicest *Régie* cigarettes with the rose-petal tips."

"If you do," smiled Markham, "he'll probably arrest you as a suspicious character."

We had drawn up abruptly in front of an old brownstone residence on the upper side of Forty-eighth Street, near Sixth Avenue. It was a house of the better class, built on a twenty-five-foot lot in a day when permanency and beauty were still matters of consideration among the city's architects. The design was conventional, to accord with the other houses in the block, but a touch of luxury and individuality was to be seen in its decorative copings and in the stone carvings about the entrance and above the windows.

There was a shallow paved areaway between the street line and the front elevation of the house; but this was enclosed in a high iron railing, and the only entrance was by way of the front door, which was about six feet above the street level at the top of a flight of ten broad stone stairs. Between the entrance and the right-hand wall were two spacious windows covered with heavy iron *grilles.*

A considerable crowd of morbid onlookers had gathered in front of the house; and on the steps lounged several alert-looking young men whom I took to be newspaper reporters. The door of our taxicab was opened by a uniformed patrolman who saluted Markham with exaggerated respect and ostentatiously cleared a passage for us through the gaping throng of idlers. Another uniformed patrolman stood in the little vestibule and, on recognizing Markham, held the outer door open for us and saluted with great dignity.

"*Ave, Cæsar, te salutamus,*" whispered Vance, grinning.

"Be quiet," Markham grumbled. "I've got troubles enough without your garbled quotations."

As we passed through the massive carved-oak front door into the main hallway, we were met by Assistant District Attorney Dinwiddie, a serious, swarthy young man with a prematurely lined face, whose appearance gave one the impression that most of the woes of humanity were resting upon his shoulders.

"Good morning, Chief," he greeted Markham, with eager relief. "I'm damned glad you've got here. This case'll rip things wide open. Cut-and-dried murder, and not a lead."

Markham nodded gloomily, and looked past him into the living room.

"Who's here?" he asked.

"The whole works, from the Chief Inspector down," Dinwiddie told him, with a hopeless shrug, as if the fact boded ill for all concerned.

At that moment a tall, massive, middle-aged man with a pink complexion and a closely cropped white moustache, appeared in the doorway of the living-room. On seeing Markham he came forward stiffly with outstretched hand. I recognized him at once as Chief Inspector O'Brien, who was in command of the entire Police Department. Dignified greetings were exchanged between him and Markham, and then Vance and I were introduced to him. Inspector O'Brien gave us each a curt, silent nod and turned back to the living room, with Markham, Dinwiddie, Vance, and myself following.

The room, which was entered by a wide double door about ten feet down the hall, was a spacious one, almost square, and with high ceilings. Two windows gave on the street; and on the extreme right of the north wall, opposite to the front of the house, was another window opening on a paved court. To the left of this window were the sliding doors leading into the dining room at the rear.

The room presented an appearance of garish opulence. About the walls hung several elaborately framed paintings of racehorses and a number of mounted hunting trophies. A highly colored oriental rug covered nearly the entire floor. In the middle of the east wall, facing the door, was an ornate fireplace and carved marble mantel. Placed diagonally in the corner on the right stood a walnut upright piano with copper trimmings. Then there was a mahogany bookcase with glass doors and figured curtains, a sprawling tapestried davenport, a squat Venetian tabouret with inlaid mother of pearl, a teakwood stand containing a large brass samovar, and a buhl-topped center table nearly six feet long. At the side of the table nearest the hallway, with its back to the front windows, stood a large wicker lounge chair with a high, fan-shaped back.

In this chair reposed the body of Alvin Benson.

Though I had served two years at the front in the World War and had seen death in many terrible guises, I could not repress a strong sense of revulsion at the sight of this murdered man. In France death had seemed an inevitable part of my daily routine, but here all the organisms of environment were opposed to the idea of fatal violence. The bright June sunshine was pouring into the room, and through the open windows came the continuous din of the city's noises, which, for all their cacophony, are associated with peace and security and the orderly social processes of life.

Benson's body was reclining in the chair in an attitude so natural that one almost expected him to turn to us and ask

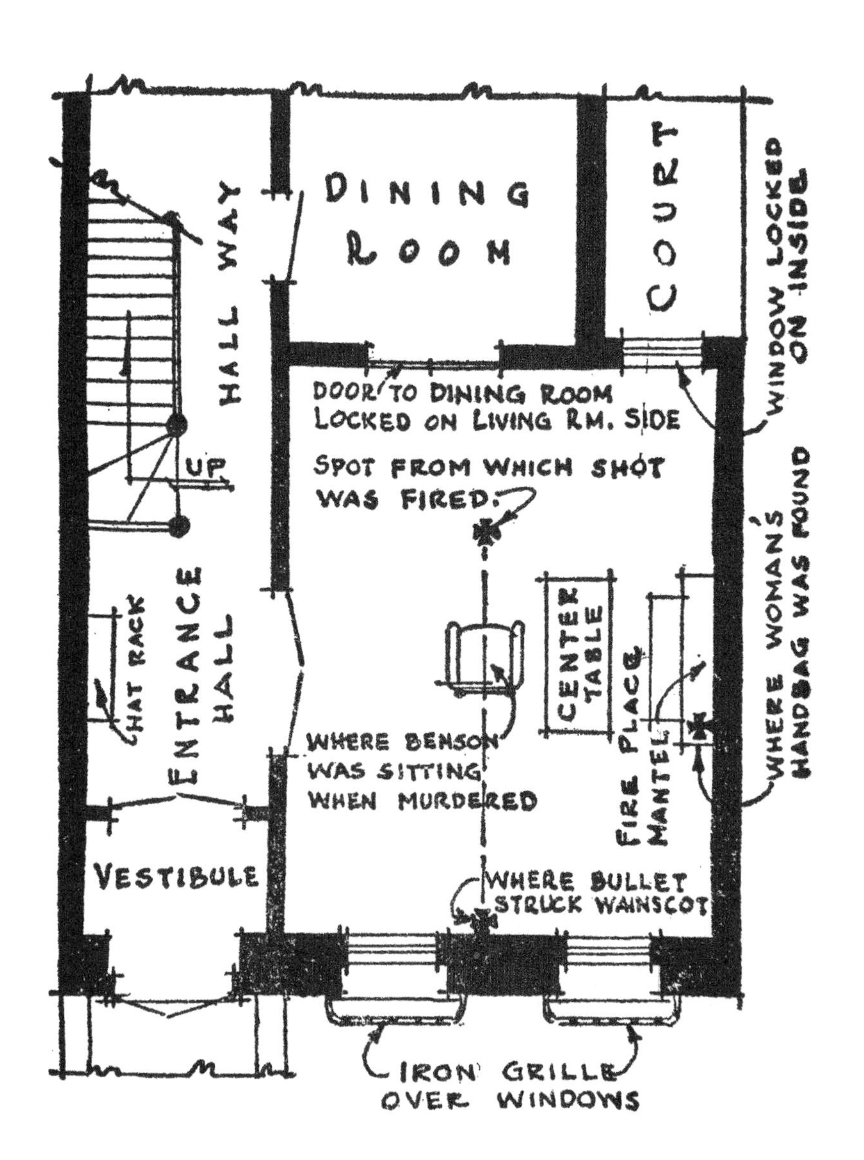


WEST 48TH. STREET

why we were intruding upon his privacy. His head was resting against the chair's back. His right leg was crossed over his left in a position of comfortable relaxation. His right arm was resting easily on the center table, and his left arm lay along the chair's arm. But that which most strikingly gave his attitude its appearance of naturalness was a small book which he held in his right hand with his thumb still marking the place where he had evidently been reading.*

He had been shot through the forehead from in front; and the small circular bullet mark was now almost black as a result of the coagulation of the blood. A large dark spot on the rug at the rear of the chair indicated the extent of the hemorrhage caused by the grinding passage of the bullet through his brain. Had it not been for these grisly indications, one might have thought that he had merely paused momentarily in his reading to lean back and rest.

He was attired in an old smoking jacket and red felt bedroom slippers but still wore his dress trousers and evening shirt, though he was collarless, and the neck band of the shirt had been unbuttoned as if for comfort. He was not an attractive man physically, being almost completely bald and more than a little stout. His face was flabby, and the puffiness of his neck was doubly conspicuous without its confining collar. With a slight shudder of distaste I ended my brief contemplation of him and turned to the other occupants of the room.

Two burly fellows with large hands and feet, their black felt hats pushed far back on their heads, were minutely inspecting the iron grill-work over the front windows. They seemed to be giving particular attention to the points where the bars were cemented into the masonry; and one of them had just taken hold of a *grille* with both hands and was shaking it, simian-wise, as if to test its strength. Another man, of medium height and dapper

---

* *The book was O. Henry's* Strictly Business, *and the place at which it was being held open was, curiously enough, the story entitled "A Municipal Report."*

appearance, with a small blond moustache, was bending over in front of the grate looking intently, so it seemed, at the dusty gas logs. On the far side of the table a thickset man in blue serge and a derby hat, stood with arms akimbo scrutinizing the silent figure in the chair. His eyes, hard and pale blue, were narrowed, and his square prognathous jaw was rigidly set. He was gazing with rapt intensity at Benson's body, as though he hoped, by the sheer power of concentration, to probe the secret of the murder.

Another man, of unusual mien, was standing before the rear window, with a jeweller's magnifying glass in his eye, inspecting a small object held in the palm of his hand. From pictures I had seen of him I knew he was Captain Carl Hagedorn, the most famous firearms expert in America. He was a large, cumbersome, broad-shouldered man of about fifty; and his black shiny clothes were several sizes too large for him. His coat hitched up behind, and in front hung halfway down to his knees; and his trousers were baggy and lay over his ankles in grotesquely comic folds. His head was round and abnormally large, and his ears seemed sunken into his skull. His mouth was entirely hidden by a scraggly, grey-shot moustache, all the hairs of which grew downward, forming a kind of lambrequin to his lips. Captain Hagedorn had been connected with the New York Police Department for thirty years, and though his appearance and manner were ridiculed at Headquarters, he was profoundly respected. His word on any point pertaining to firearms and gunshot wounds was accepted as final by Headquarters men.

In the rear of the room, near the dining room door, stood two other men talking earnestly together. One was Inspector William M. Moran, Commanding Officer of the Detective Bureau; the other, Sergeant Ernest Heath of the Homicide Bureau, of whom Markham had already spoken to us.

As we entered the room in the wake of Chief Inspector O'Brien everyone ceased his occupation for a moment and looked at the District Attorney in a spirit of uneasy, but respectful, recognition. Only Captain Hagedorn, after a cursory squint at Markham, returned to the inspection of the tiny object in his hand, with an abstracted unconcern which brought a faint smile to Vance's lips.

Inspector Moran and Sergeant Heath came forward with stolid dignity; and after the ceremony of handshaking (which I later observed to be a kind of religious rite among the police and the members of the District Attorney's staff), Markham introduced Vance and me and briefly explained our presence. The inspector bowed pleasantly to indicate his acceptance of the intrusion, but I noticed that Heath ignored Markham's explanation and proceeded to treat us as if we were nonexistent.

Inspector Moran was a man of different quality from the others in the room. He was about sixty, with white hair and a brown moustache, and was immaculately dressed. He looked more like a successful Wall Street broker of the better class than a police official.*

"I've assigned Sergeant Heath to the case, Mr. Markham," he explained in a low, well-modulated voice. "It looks as though we are in for a bit of trouble before it's finished. Even the Chief Inspector thought it warranted his lending the moral support of his presence to the preliminary rounds. He has been here since eight o'clock."

Inspector O'Brien had left us immediately upon entering the room, and now stood between the front windows, watching the proceedings with a grave, indecipherable face.

"Well, I think I'll be going," Moran added. "They had me out of bed at seven-thirty, and I haven't had any breakfast yet. I won't be needed anyway now that you're here... Good morning." And again he shook hands.

When he had gone, Markham turned to the Assistant District Attorney.

"Look after these two gentlemen, will you, Dinwiddie? They're babes in the wood and want to see how these affairs

---

* *Inspector Moran (as I learned later) had once been the president of a large upstate bank that had failed during the panic of 1907, and during the Gaynor Administration had been seriously considered for the post of Police Commissioner.*

work. Explain things to them while I have a little confab with Sergeant Heath."

Dinwiddie accepted the assignment eagerly. I think he was glad of the opportunity to have someone to talk to by way of venting his pent-up excitement.

As the three of us turned rather instinctively toward the body of the murdered man—he was, after all, the hub of this tragic drama—I heard Heath say in a sullen voice:

"I suppose you'll take charge now, Mr. Markham."

Dinwiddie and Vance were talking together, and I watched Markham with interest after what he had told us of the rivalry between the Police Department and the District Attorney's office.

Markham looked at Heath with a slow, gracious smile and shook his head.

"No, Sergeant," he replied. "I'm here to work with you, and I want that relationship understood from the outset. In fact, I wouldn't be here now if Major Benson hadn't 'phoned me and asked me to lend a hand. And I particularly want my name kept out of it. It's pretty generally known—and if it isn't, it will be—that the Major is an old friend of mine; so, it will be better all round if my connection with the case is kept quiet."

Heath murmured something I did not catch, but I could see that he had, in large measure, been placated. He, in common with all other men who were acquainted with Markham, knew his word was good; and he personally liked the District Attorney.

"If there's any credit coming from this affair," Markham went on, "the Police Department is to get it; therefore I think it best for you to see the reporters… And, by the way," he added good-naturedly, "if there's any blame coming, you fellows will have to bear that, too."

"Fair enough," assented Heath.

"And now, Sergeant, let's get to work," said Markham.

# CHAPTER THREE

## *A Lady's Hand-Bag*

*(Friday, June 14; 9.30 a.m.)*

THE DISTRICT ATTORNEY and Heath walked up to the body, and stood regarding it.

"You see," Heath explained; "he was shot directly from the front. A pretty powerful shot, too, for the bullet passed through the head and struck the woodwork over there by the window." He pointed to a place on the wainscot a short distance from the floor near the drapery of the window nearest the hallway. "We found the expelled shell, and Captain Hagedorn's got the bullet."

He turned to the firearms expert.

"How about it, Captain? Anything special?"

Hagedorn raised his head slowly and gave Heath a myopic frown. Then, after a few awkward movements, he answered with unhurried precision:

"A forty-five army bullet—Colt automatic."

"Any idea how close to Benson the gun was held?" asked Markham.

"Yes, sir, I have," Hagedorn replied, in his ponderous monotone. "Between five and six feet—probably."

Heath snorted.

" 'Probably,' " he repeated to Markham with good-natured contempt. "You can bank on it if the Captain says so... You see, sir, nothing smaller than a forty-four or forty-five will stop a man, and these steel-capped army bullets go through a human skull like it was cheese. But in order to carry straight to the woodwork the gun had to be held pretty close; and as there aren't any powder marks on the face, it's a safe bet to take the Captain's figures as to distance."

At this point we heard the front door open and close, and Dr. Doremus, the Chief Medical Examiner, accompanied by his assistant, bustled in. He shook hands with Markham and Inspector O'Brien, and gave Heath a friendly salutation.

"Sorry I couldn't get here sooner," he apologized.

He was a nervous man with a heavily seamed face and the manner of a real estate salesman.

"What have we got here?" he asked, in the same breath, making a wry face at the body in the chair.

"You tell us, Doc," retorted Heath.

Dr. Doremus approached the murdered man with a callous indifference indicative of a long process of hardening. He first inspected the face closely—he was, I imagine, looking for powder marks. Then he glanced at the bullet hole in the forehead and at the ragged wound in the back of the head. Next he moved the dead man's arm, bent the fingers, and pushed the head a little to the side. Having satisfied himself as to the state of *rigor mortis*, he turned to Heath.

"Can we get him on the settee there?"

Heath looked at Markham inquiringly.

"All through, sir?"

Markham nodded, and Heath beckoned to the two men at the front windows and ordered the body placed on the davenport. It retained its sitting posture, due to the hardening of the muscles after death, until the doctor and his assistant straightened out the limbs. The body was then undressed, and Dr. Doremus examined it carefully for other wounds. He paid particular attention to the arms; and he opened both hands wide and scrutinized the palms. At length he straightened up and wiped his hands on a large colored silk handkerchief.

"Shot through the left frontal," he announced. "Direct angle of fire. Bullet passed completely through the skull. Exit wound in the left occipital region—base of skull,—you found the bullet, didn't you? He was awake when shot, and death was immediate—probably never knew what hit him... He's been dead about—well, I should judge, eight hours; maybe longer."

"How about twelve-thirty for the exact time?" asked Heath.

The doctor looked at his watch.

"Fits O.K.... Anything else?"

No one answered, and after a slight pause the Chief Inspector spoke.

"We'd like a postmortem report today, Doctor."

"That'll be all right," Dr. Doremus answered, snapping shut his medical case and handing it to his assistant. "But get the body to the Mortuary as soon as you can."

After a brief handshaking ceremony, he went out hurriedly.

Heath turned to the detective who had been standing by the table when we entered.

"Burke, you 'phone Headquarters to call for the body—and tell 'em to get a move on. Then go back to the office and wait for me."

Burke saluted and disappeared.

Heath then addressed one of the two men who had been inspecting the *grilles* of the front windows.

"How about that ironwork, Snitkin?"

"No chance, Sergeant," was the answer. "Strong as a jail—both of 'em. Nobody never got in through those windows."

"Very good," Heath told him. "Now you two fellows chase along with Burke."

When they had gone, the dapper man in the blue serge suit and derby, whose sphere of activity had seemed to be the fireplace, laid two cigarette butts on the table.

"I found these under the gas logs, Sergeant," he explained unenthusiastically. "Not much, but there's nothing else laying around."

"All right, Emery." Heath gave the butts a disgruntled look. "You needn't wait, either. I'll see you at the office later."

Hagedorn came ponderously forward.

"I guess I'll be getting along, too," he rumbled. "But I'm going to keep this bullet a while. It's got some peculiar rifling marks on it. You don't want it specially, do you, Sergeant?"

Heath smiled tolerantly.

"What'll I do with it, Captain? You keep it. But don't you dare lose it."

"I won't lose it," Hagedorn assured him, with stodgy seriousness; and, without so much as a glance at either the District Attorney or the Chief Inspector, he waddled from the room with a slightly rolling movement which suggested that of some huge amphibious mammal.

Vance, who was standing beside me near the door, turned and followed Hagedorn into the hall. The two stood talking in low tones for several minutes. Vance appeared to be asking questions, and although I was not close enough to hear their conversation, I caught several words and phrases—"trajectory," "muzzle velocity," "angle of fire," "impetus," "impact," "deflection," and the like—and wondered what on earth had prompted this strange interrogation.

As Vance was thanking Hagedorn for his information Inspector O'Brien entered the hall.

"Learning fast?" he asked, smiling patronizingly at Vance. Then, without waiting for a reply: "Come along, Captain; I'll drive you down town."

Markham heard him.

"Have you got room for Dinwiddie, too, Inspector?"

"Plenty, Mr. Markham."

The three of them went out.

Vance and I were now left alone in the room with Heath and the District Attorney, and, as if by common impulse, we all settled ourselves in chairs, Vance taking one near the dining room door directly facing the chair in which Benson had been murdered.

I had been keenly interested in Vance's manner and actions from the moment of his arrival at the house. When he had first entered the room he had adjusted his monocle carefully—an act which, despite his air of passivity, I recognized as an indication of interest. When his mind was alert and he wished to take on external impressions quickly, he invariably brought out his monocle. He could see adequately enough without it, and his use of it, I had observed, was largely the result of an intellectual dictate. The added clarity of vision it gave him seemed subtly to affect his clarity of mind.*

At first he had looked over the room incuriously and watched the proceedings with bored apathy; but during Heath's brief questioning of his subordinates, an expression of cynical amusement had appeared on his face. Following a few general queries to Assistant District Attorney Dinwiddie, he had sauntered, with apparent aimlessness, about the room, looking at the various articles and occasionally shifting his gaze back and forth between different pieces of furniture. At length he had stooped down and inspected the mark made by the bullet on the wainscot; and once he had gone to the door and looked up and down the hall.

The only thing that had seemed to hold his attention to any extent was the body itself. He had stood before it for several minutes, studying its position, and had even bent over the outstretched arm on the table as if to see just how the

---

* *Vance's eyes were slightly bifocal. His right eye was 1.2 astigmatic, whereas his left eye was practically normal.*

dead man's hand was holding the book. The crossed position of the legs, however, had attracted him most, and he had stood studying them for a considerable time. Finally, he had returned his monocle to his waistcoat pocket, and joined Dinwiddie and me near the door, where he had stood, watching Heath and the other detectives with lazy indifference, until the departure of Captain Hagedorn.

The four of us had no more than taken seats when the patrolman stationed in the vestibule appeared at the door.

"There's a man from the local precinct station here, sir," he announced, "who wants to see the officer in charge. Shall I send him in?"

Heath nodded curtly, and a moment later a large red-faced Irishman, in civilian clothes, stood before us. He saluted Heath, but on recognizing the District Attorney, made Markham the recipient of his report.

"I'm Officer McLaughlin, sir—West Forty-seventh Street station," he informed us; "and I was on duty on this beat last night. Around midnight, I guess it was, there was a big grey Cadillac standing in front of this house—I noticed it particular, because it had a lot of fishing tackle sticking out the back, and all of its lights were on. When I heard of the crime this morning, I reported the car to the station sergeant, and he sent me around to tell you about it."

"Excellent," Markham commented; and then, with a nod, referred the matter to Heath.

"May be something in it," the latter admitted dubiously. "How long would you say the car was here, officer?"

"A good half hour anyway. It was here before twelve, and when I come back at twelve-thirty or thereabouts, it was still here. But the next time I come by, it was gone."

"You saw nothing else? Nobody in the car, or anyone hanging around who might have been the owner?"

"No, sir, I did not."

Several other questions of a similar nature were asked him; but nothing more could be learned, and he was dismissed.

"Anyway," remarked Heath, "the car story will be good stuff to hand the reporters."

Vance had sat through the questioning of McLaughlin with drowsy inattention—I doubt if he even heard more than the first few words of the officer's report—and now, with a stifled yawn, he rose and, sauntering to the center table, picked up one of the cigarette butts that had been found in the fireplace. After rolling it between his thumb and forefinger and scrutinizing the tip, he ripped the paper open with his thumbnail and held the exposed tobacco to his nose.

Heath, who had been watching him gloweringly, leaned suddenly forward in his chair.

"What are you doing there?" he demanded, in a tone of surly truculence.

Vance lifted his eyes in decorous astonishment.

"Merely smelling of the tobacco," he replied, with condescending unconcern. "It's rather mild, y' know, but delicately blended."

The muscles in Heath's cheeks worked angrily. "Well, you'd better put it down, sir," he advised. Then he looked Vance up and down. "Tobacco expert?" he asked, with ill-disguised sarcasm.

"Oh, dear no." Vance's voice was dulcet. "My specialty is scarab-cartouches of the Ptolemaic dynasties."

Markham interposed diplomatically.

"You really shouldn't touch anything around here, Vance, at this stage of the game. You never know what'll turn out to be important. Those cigarette stubs may quite possibly be significant evidence."

"Evidence?" repeated Vance sweetly. "My word! You don't say, really! Most amusin'!"

Markham was plainly annoyed; and Heath was boiling inwardly but made no further comment: he even forced a mirthless smile. He evidently felt that he had been a little too abrupt with this friend of the District Attorney's, however much the friend might have deserved being reprimanded.

Heath, however, was no sycophant in the presence of his superiors. He knew his worth and lived up to it with his whole energy, discharging the tasks to which he was assigned with a dogged indifference to his own political well-being. This stubbornness of spirit, and the solidity of character it implied, were respected and valued by the men over him.

He was a large, powerful man but agile and graceful in his movements, like a highly trained boxer. He had hard blue eyes, remarkably bright and penetrating, a small nose, a broad, oval chin, and a stern, straight mouth with lips that appeared always compressed. His hair, which, though he was well along in his forties, was without a trace of greyness, was cropped about the edges and stood upright in a short bristly pompadour. His voice had an aggressive resonance, but he rarely blustered. In many ways he accorded with the conventional notion of what a detective is like. But there was something more to the man's personality, an added capability and strength, as it were; and as I sat watching him that morning I felt myself unconsciously admiring him, despite his very obvious limitations.

"What's the exact situation, Sergeant?" Markham asked. "Dinwiddie gave me only the barest facts."

Heath cleared his throat.

"We got the word a little before seven. Benson's housekeeper, a Mrs. Platz, called up the local station and reported that she'd found him dead, and asked that somebody be sent over at once. The message, of course, was relayed to Headquarters. I wasn't there at the time, but Burke and Emery were on duty, and after notifying Inspector Moran, they came on up here. Several of the men from the local station were already on the job doing the usual nosing about. When the Inspector had got here and looked the situation over, he telephoned me to hurry along. When I arrived, the local men had gone, and three more men from the Homicide Bureau had joined Burke and Emery. The Inspector also 'phoned Captain Hagedorn—he thought the case big enough to call him in on it at once—and the Captain had just got here when you arrived. Mr. Dinwiddie had come in right after the Inspector and 'phoned you at once. Chief Inspector O'Brien came along a little ahead of me. I questioned the Platz woman right off; and my men were looking the place over when you showed up."

"Where's this Mrs. Platz now?" asked Markham.

"Upstairs being watched by one of the local men. She lives in the house."

"Why did you mention the specific hour of twelve-thirty to the doctor?"

"Platz told me she heard a report at that time, which I thought might have been the shot. I guess now it *was* the shot—it checks up with a number of things."

"I think we'd better have another talk with Mrs. Platz," Markham suggested. "But first: did you find anything suggestive in the room here—anything to go on?"

Heath hesitated almost imperceptibly; then he drew from his coat pocket a woman's handbag and a pair of long white kid gloves, and tossed them on the table in front of the District Attorney.

"Only these," he said. "One of the local men found them on the end of the mantel over there."

After a casual inspection of the gloves, Markham opened the handbag and turned its contents out onto the table. I came forward and looked on, but Vance remained in his chair, placidly smoking a cigarette.

The handbag was of fine gold mesh with a catch set with small sapphires. It was unusually small, and obviously designed only for evening wear. The objects which it had held, and which Markham was now inspecting, consisted of a flat watered-silk cigarette case, a small gold phial of Roger and Gallet's *Fleurs d'Amour* perfume, a *cloisonné* vanity-compact, a short delicate cigarette holder of inlaid amber, a gold-cased lipstick, a small embroidered French-linen handkerchief with "M. St.C." monogrammed in the corner, and a Yale latchkey.

"This ought to give us a good lead," said Markham, indicating the handkerchief. "I suppose you went over the articles carefully, Sergeant."

Heath nodded.

"Yes; and I imagine the bag belongs to the woman Benson was out with last night. The housekeeper told me he had an appointment and went out to dinner in his dress clothes. She didn't hear Benson when he came back, though. Anyway, we ought to be able to run down Miss 'M. St.C.' without much trouble."

Markham had taken up the cigarette case again, and as he held it upside down a little shower of loose dried tobacco fell onto the table.

Heath stood up suddenly.

"Maybe those cigarettes came out of that case," he suggested. He picked up the intact butt and looked at it. "It's a lady's cigarette, all right. It looks as though it might have been smoked in a holder, too."

"I beg to differ with you, Sergeant," drawled Vance. "You'll forgive me, I'm sure. But there's a bit of lip rouge on the end of the cigarette. It's hard to see, on account of the gold tip."

Heath looked at Vance sharply; he was too much surprised to be resentful. After a closer inspection of the cigarette, he turned again to Vance.

"Perhaps you could also tell us from these tobacco grains, if the cigarettes came from this case," he suggested, with gruff irony.

"One never knows, does one?" Vance replied, indolently rising.

Picking up the case, he pressed it wide open and tapped it on the table. Then he looked into it closely, and a humorous smile twitched the corners of his mouth. Putting his forefinger deep into the case, he drew out a small cigarette which had evidently been wedged flat along the bottom of the pocket.

"My olfact'ry gifts won't be necess'ry now," he said. "It is apparent even to the naked eye that the cigarettes are, to speak loosely, identical—eh what, Sergeant?"

Heath grinned good-naturedly.

"That's one on us, Mr. Markham." And he carefully put the cigarette and the stub in an envelope, which he marked and pocketed.

"You now see, Vance," observed Markham, "the importance of those cigarette butts."

"Can't say that I do," responded the other. "Of what possible value is a cigarette butt? You can't smoke it, y' know."

"It's evidence, my dear fellow," explained Markham patiently. "One knows that the owner of this bag returned with Benson last night and remained long enough to smoke two cigarettes."

Vance lifted his eyebrows in mock amazement.

"One does, does one? Fancy that, now."

"It only remains to locate her," interjected Heath.

"She's a rather decided brunette, at any rate—if that fact will facilitate your quest any," said Vance easily; "though why you should desire to annoy the lady, I can't for the life of me imagine—really I can't, don't y' know."

"Why do you say she's a brunette?" asked Markham.

"Well, if she isn't," Vance told him, sinking listlessly back in his chair, "then she should consult a cosmetician as to the proper way to make up. I see she uses 'Rachel' powder and Guerlain's dark lipstick. And it simply isn't done among blondes, old dear."

"I defer, of course, to your expert opinion," smiled Markham. Then, to Heath: "I guess we'll have to look for a brunette, Sergeant."

"It's all right with me," agreed Heath jocularly. By this time, I think, he had entirely forgiven Vance for destroying the cigarette butt.

If you love Golden Age mysteries and are perhaps ready for something more traditional after Philo Vance's citified airs, may we suggest the Henry Tibbett series, by Patricia Moyes? The Tibbett novels, though more recent, are classics in the "steady English Detective Inspector knows what's what" mode, made more charming by the good Inspector's astute and lovable wife. We've included the first few chapters of *Dead Men Don't Ski* (Henry Tibbett #1), and we hope you enjoy meeting Henry and Emmy.

# DEAD MEN DON'T SKI

## CHAPTER ONE

**IT WAS JUST NINE O'CLOCK** on a cold and clammy January morning when Chief Inspector Henry Tibbett's taxi drew up outside the uninviting cavern of Victoria Station. From the suburban lines the Saturday morning hordes of office-bound workers streamed anxiously through the barriers to bus and underground—pale, strained faces, perpetually in a hurry, perpetually late: but here, at this side-entrance that led into a sort of warehouse fitted with an imposing array of weighing platforms, were assembled a group of people who looked as paradoxical at that hour and place as a troupe of Nautch girls at the Athenæum. They were not all young, Henry noted with relief, though the average age was certainly under thirty: but young or middle-aged, male or female, all were unanimous in their defiant sartorial abandon—the tightest trousers, the gaudiest sweaters, the heaviest boots, the silliest knitted hats that ever burst from the overcharged imagination of a Winter Sports Department. The faces were pale, true, but—Henry noted with a sinking heart—quite aggressively merry and free from any sign of stress: the voices were unnaturally loud and friendly. The whole dingy place had the air of a monstrous end-of-term party.

"Will you pay the taxi, darling, while I cope with the luggage?" Emmy's amused voice recalled Henry from his fascinated appraisal of the dog beneath the Englishman's skin.

"Yes, yes, of course. No, don't try to lift it… I'll get a porter…"

The taxi grumbled on its way, and Henry was gratified to see that a small porter with the face of a malevolent monkey, who had been lounging by the wall rolling a cigarette with maddening deliberation, now came forward to offer his services.

"Santa Chiara, sir? 'Ave you got skis to register through?" The porter almost smiled.

"No," said Henry. "We're hiring them out there. We've just got—"

But the porter had abruptly lost interest, and transferred his attentions to a taxi which had just drawn up, and which most evidently had skis to register through. A man with a smooth red face and unmistakably military bearing was getting out, followed by a bristling forest of skis and sticks, and a large woman with a bad-tempered expression. As the wizened porter swept the skis and sticks expertly onto his trolley, Henry caught sight of a boldly written label—"Col. Buckfast, Albergo Bella Vista, Santa Chiara, Italy. Via Innsbruck."

"They're at our hotel," he muttered miserably to Emmy.

She grinned. "Never mind. So are those nice youngsters over there."

Henry turned to see a group of three young people, who were certainly outstanding as far as good looks were concerned. The girl was about twenty years old, Henry judged, with short-cropped hair and brilliantly candid blue eyes. One of the young men was quite remarkably handsome, fair and grey-eyed, with very beautiful hands—at once strong and sensitive ("I've seen his picture somewhere," whispered Emmy). The other youth did not quite achieve the standard of physical perfection set by the rest of the party—he was tall and thin, with a beak of a nose and dark hair that was rather too long—but he made up for it by the dazzling appearance of his clothes. His trousers, skintight, were pale blue, like a Ruritanian officer's in a musical comedy: his sweater was the yellow of egg yolks, with geranium-red reindeer circumnavigating it just below the armpits: his woollen cap, in shape like the ultimate decoration of a cream cake, was royal blue. At the moment, he was laughing uproariously, slapping a spindly blue leg with a bamboo ski-stick.

"Good heavens," said Henry. "That's Jimmy Passendell—old Raven's youngest son. He's..." He hesitated, because the idea seemed ludicrous—"...he's a member of Lloyd's."

At that moment a burly porter, evidently deciding that the time had come to clear the pavement for newcomers, seized Henry's luggage unceremoniously, tucking a suitcase under each arm and picking up the other two with effortless ease; and with a bellow of "Where to, sir?" he disappeared into the station without waiting for an answer.

Henry and Emmy trotted dutifully after him, and found themselves beside a giant weighing machine, which at the moment was laden with skis.

"Which registered?" asked the porter laconically, twirling Emmy's dressing case playfully in his huge hand.

"I'm afraid I don't quite understand about..." Henry began, feeling almost unbearably foolish. Everybody else obviously understood.

"Registered goes straight through—Customs here—don't see it again till Innsbruck," said the porter, pityingly.

"We'll register the two big ones," said Emmy firmly.

For the next few minutes Henry trotted between luggage, porter, and ticket office like a flustered but conscientious mother bird intent on satisfying her brood's craving for worms—the worms in this case being those cryptic bits of paper which railway officials delight to stamp, perforate, clip, and shake their heads over. Eventually all was done, the Customs cleared, and Henry and Emmy were safely installed, with the two smaller cases, in the corner seats reserved for their journey to Dover.

Henry sank back with a sigh in which relief was not unmingled with apprehension. For the moment they had the carriage to themselves, and the screaming chaos of the luggage shed had given way to the sounds of muted excitement which precede the departure of a long-distance train.

"I suppose the Yard know what they're doing," said Henry. "Because I don't. I wish we'd decided to do our skiing somewhere else."

"Nonsense," said Emmy. "I'm enjoying myself. And I haven't seen anybody in the least suspicious yet, except the taxi driver and that screwed-up porter."

Henry gave her a reproving, walls-have-ears glance, and opened his *Times*, turning gratefully to the civilised solace of the crossword puzzle.

Henry Tibbett was not a man who looked like a great detective. In fact, as he would be the first to point out, he was not a great detective, but a conscientious and observant policeman, with an occasional flair for intuitive detection which he called "my nose." There were very few of his superiors who were not prepared to listen, and to take appropriate action, when Henry said, suddenly, "My nose tells me we're on the wrong lines. Why not tackle it this way?" The actual nose in question was as pleasant—and as unremarkable—as the rest of Henry Tibbett. A small man, sandy-haired and with pale eyebrows and lashes which emphasised his general air of timidity, he had spent most of his forty-eight years trying to avoid trouble—with a conspicuous lack of success.

"It's not my fault," he once remarked plaintively to Emmy, "that things always seem to blow up at my feet." The consequence was that he had a wide and quite undeserved reputation as a desperado, an adventurer who hid his bravura under a mask of meekness: and his repeated assertions that he only wanted to lead a quiet life naturally fed the flames of this rumour.

Emmy, of course, knew Henry as he really was—and knew that the truth about him lay somewhere between the swashbuckling figure of his subordinates' imagination, and the mild and mousy character he protested himself to be. She knew, too—and it reassured and comforted her—that Henry needed her placid strength and good humour as much as he needed food and drink. She was forty now—not as slim as she had been, but with a pleasantly curving figure and a pleasantly intelligent face. Her most striking feature was her skin, which was wonderfully white and fair, a piquant contrast to her curly black hair.

She looked at her watch. "We'll be off soon" she said. "I wonder who else is in our carriage."

They very soon found out. Mrs. Buckfast's voice could be heard raised in complaint a full corridor away, before she finally entered the carriage like a man-o'-war under full sail. Her seat, naturally, was the wrong one. She had definitely been given to understand that she would have a corner seat, facing the engine.

"I can only say, Arthur," she said, her eyes fixed on Henry, "that reservations seem to mean absolutely nothing to *some people*." Unhappily, Henry offered her his seat. Mrs. Buckfast started, as though seeing him for the first time; then accepted the seat with a bad grace.

Soon a cheerful commotion in the corridor heralded the arrival of Jimmy Passendell and his party. ("Seven in a carriage is *far too many*," Mrs. Buckfast announced to nobody in particular.) The girl became engrossed in the latest copy of the *Tatler*. Colonel Buckfast nodded briefly at the handsome young man, and said, "Back again this year, eh? Had a feeling you might be." The young man remarked that he hoped the snow would be as good as it had been the year before, and proceeded to cope expertly with the baggage, even coaxing a sour smile from Mrs. Buckfast by lifting a large number of small cases up to the rack for her. Jimmy Passendell immediately counteracted this momentary lightening of the atmosphere by producing a mouth organ and inviting the company to join him in the chorus of "Dear Old Pals."

"After all," he remarked brightly, "we soon shall be—we're all going to Santa Chiara, aren't we—to the Bella Vista." After a pause, he added, "Yippee!" The pretty blonde giggled; the handsome youth looked uncomfortable; the Colonel and Henry retreated still further behind their respective *Times*; Emmy laughed outright, and produced a tin of digestive biscuits, which she offered to all and sundry. The young people fell on them with whoops of delight, and for a time conversation was mercifully replaced by a contented munching. The train moved slowly out of Victoria into the mist.

The channel was grey and cold, but calm. The skiers clumped cheerfully up the gangplank in their resounding boots, and made a concerted dash for the warmth and solace of the saloon, dining room or bar according to temperament. As the steamer moved slowly away from the dockside and out of the narrow harbour entrance, Henry and Emmy had the deck to themselves. They leant over the rail, savouring the peace, the absence of strident human voices, and watching the familiar outline of the cliffs grow dim in the haze.

"There's nobody else going to Santa Chiara," said Emmy, at last. "And none of that lot look like dope-peddlers to me, whatever other failings they may have."

"The whole thing's probably a wild goose chase," said Henry. "I hope it is. Heaven knows I don't want any trouble. I want to learn to ski. After all, we are on holiday."

"Are we?" Emmy gave him a rueful smile. "Just pure coincidence that we're going to the hotel which Interpol thinks is a smugglers' den?"

"It was just my luck to pick that particular place," said Henry, ruefully. "And when Sir John heard we were going there, I couldn't very well refuse to keep my eyes open."

"Interpol know you're going to be there, though, don't they?"

"Yes—unofficially. They've no evidence against the place as yet—only suspicions. They were thinking of sending one of their own chaps to the Bella Vista as an ordinary holiday-maker, but when Sir John told them I was going anyway—"

Behind them, a familiar voice boomed. "It was *clearly* understood that we would travel first-class on the boat…"

"Let's have a drink," said Henry, hastily, and piloted Emmy down the companionway to the bar.

It was crowded, smoky and cheerful. Henry battled his way between young giants to the counter, and secured two Scotches and two hundred cigarettes for a laughable sum. By the time he had fought his way back to Emmy, she had already installed herself in the last remaining chair in the bar, and was chatting amicably to the fair girl, whose escorts were storming the bar in search of duty-free cognac.

"Oh, well done, Henry. Come and meet Miss Whittaker." Emmy seemed for some reason to stress the surname as she said it. Heavens, thought Henry. Somebody I ought to know. The girl beamed at him.

"Miss Whittaker sounds too silly," she said. "Please call me Caro."

Henry said he would be delighted to, and gave Emmy her drink. A moment later the handsome, fair-haired young man emerged from the scrum at the bar, laden with glasses and bottles. Caro fluttered into a whirl of introductions. This was darling Roger—Roger Staines, actually—who was a *frightfully* good skier and was going to shame them all—but *shame* them—and this was Henry and Emmy Tibbett and they were going to the Bella Vista—actually to the same hotel—wasn't that too extraordinary and blissful, Roger darling? Then darling Jimmy arrived with his ration of duty-free, and the party made merry, while the grey sea-miles slipped away under the keel, and the seagulls wheeled purposefully over the writhing white wake of the ship.

Calais was a scramble of porters, a perfunctory interlude with the Customs, a trek along seeming miles of platform—and eventually all five travellers were installed in Compartment E6 of a gleaming train, which had a showy plaque reading "Skisports Special" screwed to its smoking flanks. The hand-luggage was stowed away neatly above the door, and the first bottle of brandy opened (by Jimmy). The great train heaved a spluttering sigh, and pulled smoothly out of the station, heading south.

"And here we are," said Jimmy, "until tomorrow. Have some brandy."

France rolled away behind them in the already deepening dusk. Henry did his crossword; Emmy dozed; Jimmy took another swig of brandy; Caro read her magazine, and Roger stared moodily out of the window, a sulky look of bad temper ruining his impeccable profile. A small man in a leather jerkin, wearing a red armband embroidered with the words "Skisports Ltd." in yellow, put his head into the carriage.

"I'm Edward, your courier on the train," he announced brightly, blinking through thick-lensed spectacles. "Anything you want, just ask me."

"Have some brandy," said Jimmy. Edward tittered nervously, refused, and withdrew. They heard him open the door of the next compartment.

"I'm Edward, your courier on the train. If there's anything—"

"There most certainly is, my man." Mrs. Buckfast's voice rose easily above the rhythmic pulse of the wheels. They could hear it rumbling on in discontent even when the unfortunate Edward had been lured into the carriage, and the door firmly shut behind him.

A few minutes later, Caro got up and went into the corridor, where she stood leaning on the window rail, looking out at the darkening fields, the lighted farmhouse windows, the tiny country stations, as they flashed past, tossed relentlessly from future to past by the insatiable, mile-hungry monster of which they were now a part.

Emmy glanced after Caro, suddenly awake, then settled herself to sleep again. Roger Staines got up from his corner seat, and went out into the corridor, slamming the door behind him. He stood beside Caro, two backviews, inexpressive, lurching with the movement of the train. Henry could see that he was talking earnestly; that she was replying hardly at all. He could not hear what they were saying.

At five o'clock the lights of the train came on suddenly, and at six-thirty the bell sounded merrily down the corridor for First Dinner. Jimmy consulted his ticket and found that he was, indeed, due to dine at the first sitting: so, collecting Roger and Caro who were now leaning relaxedly against the carriage door, smoking and chatting idly, they went off with considerable clatter down the corridor towards the dining car.

It seemed very quiet and empty when they had gone. Henry got up and shut the door carefully. Then he said, "Roger Staines… I wish I could place him…"

"I've remembered where I've seen his picture—in the *Tatler*," said Emmy. "He's what they call a deb's delight. Look—"

She picked up the magazine that was lying on the seat where Caro had left it. It was open at one of the familiar pages which report so tirelessly on the nightlife of London, and there was a photograph of Roger and Caro toasting each other in champagne. "Miss Caroline Whittaker, Sir Charles and Lady Whittaker's lovely daughter, shares a drink and a jest at the Four Hundred with her favourite escort, Mr. Roger Staines," said the caption, coyly. Henry looked at the picture for a full minute, thoughtfully. He said again, "I wish I could place him—further back. Quite a bit further back."

"Goodness, I'm hungry," said Emmy. "Have a biscuit."

The train sped on towards the frontiers of Switzerland.

Henry and Emmy shared their table at Third Dinner with Colonel and Mrs. Buckfast. The latter, having obviously had the time of her life making mincemeat of poor Edward, was in a comparatively good humour, and agreed to take a glass of Sauternes with her fish; she even pronounced the food eatable. Her husband, evidently cheered by this unaccustomed serenity, became conversational over the coffee.

"Your first time on skis?" he asked Henry, his smooth red face aglow with affability.

"Yes, I'm a complete rabbit, I'm afraid," Henry replied. "My wife's done it before."

"Only twice," said Emmy. "I'm no good at all."

"Finest sport in the world," said the Colonel. He glanced round belligerently, as if expecting instant contradiction. Mrs. Buckfast sniffed, but said nothing. "My wife doesn't ski," he added, confidentially. "Jolly sporting of her to come out with me, year after year. I appreciate it. Of course, I'd absolutely understand if she wanted to stay behind and let me go alone…" His voice took on a wistful note.

"The mountain air is good for me," said Mrs. Buckfast, flatly. "I find ways of passing the time. It really wouldn't be fair to let poor Arthur do this trip all by himself."

"I've often told you—" he began, but she cut him short with a "Pass the sugar please, Arthur," that brooked no further discussion. There was a short silence, and then the Colonel tried again.

"Been to Santa Chiara before?" he asked.

"No."

"Interested to know what attracted you, if you're not a keen skier. Not everybody's cup of tea—hotel stuck up all by itself at the top of a chair-lift. Can't get down to the village at all after dark, you know."

"They told us the skiing was excellent," said Emmy, "and we wanted peace and quiet more than anything."

"Then you certainly picked the right spot," said Mrs. Buckfast, sourly. "I dare say," she went on, with ill-concealed curiosity, "that your husband has been working very hard. Perhaps his job is a very exhausting one."

"No more so than any other business man's," said Henry. "It's just a question of temperament, I suppose. We always like quiet holidays, off the beaten track."

"So you're a business man are you? How very interesting. In the City?"

"Not exactly," said Henry. "I work in Westminster."

Mrs. Buckfast, foiled in her attempt to extract more information about Henry's profession, went on, "Quite a distinguished party going to Santa Chiara this year. Caroline Whittaker, who had that huge ball at Claridge's last year, and the Honourable Jimmy Passendell—" her voice sank to a whisper—"Lord Raven's son you know. A bit *wild*, I understand, but charming…so charming…"

"The other lad seems pleasant, too," said Henry. "Roger Staines. I seem to know his face."

"I know nothing about him," said Mrs. Buckfast, with great firmness. "*Nothing*," she added, "whatsoever."

When Henry and Emmy got back to E6, the triple tiers of bunks had been set up, but the party showed no signs of going to bed. Jimmy had opened another bottle of brandy, and was leading the company in a variety of more or less bawdy songs. Henry and Emmy accepted a nightcap gratefully, and then suggested that they should retire to bed on the two top bunks, out of everyone's way. "Don't mind us old drears," said Emmy. "Sing as loud as you like. We enjoy it."

"Jolly decent of you," said Jimmy. "Have another drink before you embark on the perilous ascent." He said the last two words twice to make sure of getting them right. Caro was smiling now, sitting in the corner and holding hands with Roger.

In fact, the singing only went on for half an hour or so, before the whole party decided to get some rest. Caro took one of the two middle bunks, Roger and Jimmy the two lowest. Soon all was dark and quiet, except for the tiny blue bulb that burned in the ceiling, the soft breathing of the sleepers, and the thrumming wheels on the ribbon-stretch of rails. In his tiny compartment at the rear of the last coach, Edward cursed Mrs. Buckfast steadily, and with satisfaction, as he compiled his passenger list: between him and the engine driver, the sinuous length of train was all asleep.

At breakfast time next morning they were miraculously among mountains. True, the railway itself ran through wide, flat green valleys, like the beds of dried-up lakes, but all around the mountains reared proudly, fresh green giving way to grey rock, to evergreen, and finally, high above, to glistening white snow. All along the train, voices and spirits rose. The sun shone, and the snow, suddenly real, suddenly remembered, was a lure, a liberator, a potent magic. Soon, soon…

The Austrian border was left behind at half-past nine; by eleven the train was winding along the broad green valley of the River Inn, ringed by lofty mountains; at eleven-twenty precisely, the engine drew to a hissing, panting halt, and a guttural voice outside on the platform was shouting "Innsbruck! Innsbruck!" into the crisp, sunny air.

# CHAPTER TWO

AT INNSBRUCK, the compact phalanx of skiers who had travelled *en masse* from Victoria dispersed abruptly: hotel buses or small, energetic mountain trains bore them off to their respective Austrian resorts. Only the Santa Chiara party remained, suddenly rather desolate, suddenly rather out of place in their aggressive sweaters. Edward, who had come in for some uncomplimentary remarks from E6 on the train, now seemed like their last—and faithless—friend, as he hurriedly compiled his reports, and headed for his overnight lodgings in Innsbruck.

Inevitably the camaraderie of isolation manifested itself. Jimmy fetched a cup of coffee for Mrs. Buckfast, the Colonel carried Emmy's overnight case up the subway for her, Roger (with a superior command of German) collected the registered baggage, and Emmy and Caro ventured together in search of the Ladies'. Henry, feeling rather out of things, contented himself with buying enough English magazines at the bookstall to keep the whole party happy until teatime, when they were due at their destination.

Eventually all seven travellers, complete with luggage, were assembled on the correct platform to catch the Munich-Rome express, which was to carry them on the penultimate stage of their journey.

Evidently not many people wanted to exchange the exhilarating sunshine of Innsbruck for the uncertain joys of Rome in January, for nobody else was waiting for the train except an elderly couple who, Henry guessed, had been marketing in Innsbruck and were probably going no farther than Brenner, the frontier town. A few minutes before the train was due, however, a flurry of porters and expensive luggage appeared from the subway, followed by a tall and very thin man, dressed in a sort of Norfolk jacket made of bright green tweed, with a fur collar, and dark grey trousers of extreme narrowness. His face was long, and creased with deep lines of intolerance, and his lean, vulpine features were crowned incongruously by a green Tyrolean hat. With him was a girl of striking beauty: she had the face of a Florentine Madonna, with deep golden hair swept smoothly back from a broad brow and coiled on the nape of her neck. She wore pale grey ski trousers cut by a master, and a little grey jacket with a collar of snow leopard that framed her face like a cloud. Her makeup—in the Italian manner—emphasised her magnificent dark eyes, and her honey-coloured skin, while her full, lovely mouth was brushed lightly with a wild-rose pink. "Very, very expensive," Emmy whispered to Henry, as the procession of porters swept past.

Mrs. Buckfast gazed after the newcomers with uninhibited curiosity: Caro looked sheepish, suddenly conscious of her crumpled, slept-in trousers: the men, involuntarily, turned to admire, and were rewarded by a scowl from under the Tyrolean hat.

When the train pulled in, dead on time, and they had secured an empty carriage for the party without difficulty, Henry and Emmy went to the window to take a last look at Innsbruck. To their surprise, Tyrolean Hat was on the platform alone, obviously saying good-bye to the Madonna, who stood, cool and beautiful, at the window of a first-class compartment. There were kisses, protestations of affection, fussings over baggage—all of which the girl received with what looked more like dutiful resignation than enthusiasm. At one point, when the man was engaged in some sort of altercation with the porter, Henry caught her looking at him with an expression of mingled contempt and dislike which was chilling in its intensity. At last the whistle blew, and the train started. The last view of Innsbruck was of a Tyrolean hat waving, somehow pathetically, on the end of a long, thin arm.

At Brenner, after a short and amicable interlude with the Italian Customs, the whole party filed down the corridor to the dining car. The young people secured a table for four, and the Buckfasts a table for two: Henry and Emmy, arriving last, were ushered by a smiling waiter to the last table in the car—a four-seater at present occupied by one person only, the Madonna from Innsbruck. She was ordering her meal in fluent Italian, completely relaxed, spontaneous and excited—a very different person from the cool beauty of Innsbruck station. "Like a little girl out of school," Henry thought.

Throughout a delectable meal that started with *fettuccini* and meandered through *fritto misto con fagiolini* to a creamy *bel paese* cheese, there was more concentration on food than on conversation. With the coffee, however, a pleasantly replete and relaxed mood took over; the beauty made the first move by inquiring in excellent English whether Henry and Emmy were from London, and were they holidaying in Italy? They said they were.

"So am I," she said, with a ravishing smile of pure happiness. "I am Italian, you see. But my husband is Austrian, and there we must live, in Innsbruck."

"I envy you," said Henry. "It must be a beautiful city."

"Yes," said the girl, shortly. Then, smiling again—"But where do you go? Rome? Venezia? Firenze?"

"As a matter of fact, we're going to ski," said Emmy.

"Oh! I too."

"Perhaps we might even be headed for the same place," Henry suggested.

"I am sure we are not," said the beauty. "You go to Cortina, of course. All English and Americans go to Cortina."

"No," said Henry. "We're going to a little place called Santa Chiara. The Albergo Bella Vista."

To his surprise, the girl's smile faded abruptly, and for an instant a look of sheer panic crossed her face.

"Santa Chiara," she said, almost in a whisper. "I...I go there, too."

"Well how nice," said Emmy, quickly. "We must introduce ourselves. We are Henry and Emmy Tibbett."

"And I..." There was an unmistakable hesitation. Then the girl seemed to shake herself, like a puppy coming out of the sea, and her smile flashed again. "I am the Baroness von Wurtburg. But you must call me Maria-Pia. When I am in Italy, I forget that I have become an Austrian."

There was a tiny pause.

"My children are already at the Bella Vista, with the fraulein," the Baroness went on. "Hansi is eight, and Lotte six. You will meet them."

"I'll look forward to that," said Emmy, suppressing her instinct to remark that the Baroness looked ridiculously young to have an eight-year-old son. "What a pity," she added, daringly, "that your husband can't be with you, too."

Once again the panic flickered in the huge, brown eyes. "He is very busy, he cannot get away. He lets me—I mean, he likes me to return to my country each year, but he does not love Italy."

"I bet he doesn't," thought Henry, remembering the harsh features under the Tyrolean hat. He felt very sorry for the Baroness and did not know how to convey his sympathy without seeming impertinent: so he quickly paid his bill and, with friendly assurances that they would meet again soon, ushered Emmy down the dining car. As they went, Henry felt, curiously, those magnificent eyes following him. At the door he turned, to meet the Baroness's quiet, quizzical gaze. She looked him full in the eyes, and raised her head very slightly, as if in defiance. Henry, somewhat embarrassed, smiled and stepped into the swaying corridor.

At Chiusa, they made their last change. The great express rushed on southwards towards Verona, leaving the nine travellers standing in the sunshine on the little country station. All round them, the Dolomites broke the skyline with their warm, pink summits—flat rocks, pinnacled rocks, shapes whittled by wind and snow into primeval patterns of frightening strength and durability; the strength of the very old, the very tough, that has endured and will endure for time beyond thinking.

From the majesty of the mountains, a shrill tooting brought the party back to reality. There, on the opposite line, stood the most endearing train in the world. The engine—tiny, of 1870s vintage, with a tall, slender chimney and gleaming brasswork—headed just two coaches made of pale, fretted woodwork, with elaborate iron-railed observation platforms at each end. The Gothic windows of one carriage were chintz-curtained, marking them as First Class. The seats throughout were of slatted wood, with overhead racks for skis.

The young English exclaimed with delight, and made a concerted scramble for the train with their cases, closely followed by Henry and Emmy. Mrs. Buckfast remarked that it was high time they put new coaches on this line—the wooden seats were a disgrace. The Baroness, with every porter in the place at her heels, walked slowly across the flat railway track with an expression of pure love on her face. The luggage was loaded, the train shrilled its whistle, and the last lap of the journey began.

As the crow flies, it is about twenty miles from Chiusa to Santa Chiara: as the railway line winds, it is over thirty—thirty miles of tortuous, twisting track, of hairpin bends on the edge of precipices, of Stygian, smoky tunnels, of one-in-five gradients, and of some of the most breathtaking views in the world. Almost at once, they crossed the snowline, among pine trees. Soon Chiusa was just a huddle of pink and ochre houses far below. Valleys opened out gloriously, houses lost their Italianate look and became steadily more and more Alpine, with wooden balconies and eyebrows of snow on their steep, overhanging eaves. Up and up the engine puffed and snorted, nearer and nearer to the snowfields and the pink peaks. At village halts, white-aproned peasant women clambered on and off the train with baskets of eggs and precious green vegetables. Then they saw the first of the skiers. Round a steep bend, a glistening nursery slope opened up alongside the railway line, peopled with tiny, speeding figures. Excitement rose, like yeast. Up and up the train climbed, through three small resort villages, until at last a pink, onion-domed church came into view, clustered about with little houses.

"Santa Chiara," said the Baroness.

They all craned to look. The village was set at the head of a long valley—a valley of which the floor itself was over 5,000 feet above sea level. All round, the mountains stood in a semicircle, at once protective and menacing. The village seemed very small and very brave, up there in the white heights.

There was not, strictly speaking, a station. The train, showing signs of exhaustion, clanked and rumbled to a halt in the middle of a snowfield near the church: here, by a small green-painted shed, several hotel porters waited with their big luggage sledges, while skiers returning to the village for tea zoomed in an uninhibited manner across the railway line.

As the Baroness got out of the train, there was a sudden flurry as two diminutive skiers hurtled down the slope, crossed the railway tracks, and swung round in perfect parallel cristiania turns to stop dead in a spray-shower of snow beside the train.

"Mamma! Mamma!" they yelled, and the Baroness dropped her white pigskin dressing case in the snow and rushed to embrace them. The reunion was noisy, sentimental and rather moving: it was not for several moments that Henry noticed a slender, dark girl in black who had skied quietly but extremely competently down to the train behind the children, and now stood a few paces away, silently watching the outpourings of affection. She was very pale, in sharp contrast to the bronzed faces all round her, and she wore no makeup. She might have been beautiful, Henry thought, had she taken even the most elementary steps to make herself so: as it was, she seemed to concentrate on self-effacement, on anonymity.

The first greetings over, the Baroness—one arm round each of her children—beamed at the dark girl and spoke to her in German. Then she said to Emmy, "I go now with Gerda and the children for tea. The porter will take you up to the Bella Vista, so I shall see you at dinner."

She gave instructions in rapid Italian to a burly porter who had "Bella Vista" embroidered in gold on his black cap, and then, as the children skied slowly down the hill to the village street, she ran after them, laughing and teasing, trying to keep up with them. The dark-haired Gerda let them get near the bottom of the slope, then launched herself forward with a lovely, fluid movement, and took the gentle hillside in a series of superbly executed turns, gathering speed all the way, so that she was waiting for the others at the bottom, as still and silent as before.

As the porter loaded the baggage on to his sledge, Colonel Buckfast spoke for the first time that Henry could remember since Innsbruck.

"Look," he said, pointing upwards.

They all looked. Behind the railway line, the mountains reared in white splendour: by now, the sun had left the village, but lingered on the rosy peaks and on the high snowfields. Far up the mountain, where the trees thinned out, just on the dividing line between sunshine and shadow, was a single, isolated building, as dwarfed by its surroundings as a fly drowning in a churn of milk.

"The Bella Vista," said the Colonel, almost reverently.

There was a silence.

"I didn't realise it was so far up," said Emmy at last, in a small voice. "How do we get there?"

"We get there," said Mrs. Buckfast, "in a diabolical contraption known as a chair-lift. Every year I say I'll never do it again, and every year Arthur talks me into it. The very thought of it makes me feel sick. This way."

The Monte Caccia chair-lift, as all the brochures emphasise, is one of the longest in Europe. The ascent takes twenty-five minutes, during which time the chairs, on their stout overhead cable, travel smoothly and safely upwards, sometimes over steep slopes between pine trees, a mere twenty feet from the ground, more frequently over gorges and ravines which twist and tumble several hundred feet below. About once a minute, the strong metal arm which connects the chair to the cable clatters and bumps as it passes between the platforms of a massive steel pylon, set on four great concrete bases and equipped with a fire-broom and a sturdy snow-shovel in case of emergencies. For parts of the trip, the lift travels above the *pistes*, or ski runs, giving the passengers a bird's-eye view of the expertise or otherwise of the skiers below. It is one of the coldest forms of travelling known to man.

Henry was amused to see the varying reactions of the party (including himself) when faced with this ascent—especially when the first-timers grasped the fact that the chairs did not stop at any point, but continued up and down on an endless belt, so that one had to "hop" a moving chair as it passed.

The Colonel slid expertly into his chair, and waved his hand from sheer exhilaration as he soared skywards: Mrs. Buckfast took her seat competently, but with resignation, having grudgingly accepted the bright red blanket proffered by the attendant. Caro, glancing at the seemingly endless cables stretching up the mountainside, turned rather pale and remarked that she hadn't imagined it would be quite like this, and that heights made her dizzy.

"Don't worry, you'll get used to it in no time," said Roger, briskly. "There's absolutely nothing to be frightened of. I'll be in the chair right behind you. Just put down the safety bar, and then relax and enjoy the view."

Caro showed no signs of enjoying herself, but she got on to the next seat without further demur, clutching a little desperately at the vertical metal arm, like a nervous child on a roundabout, as the chair sped upwards. Roger exchanged a joke in Italian with the attendant, and had time to discover that his name was Carlo and that the lift stopped working at seven o'clock each evening, before he slipped casually into his chair, leaving the safety arm flapping. Jimmy made a loudly facetious remark about dicing with death, which made Henry suspect that he was genuinely apprehensive, but he hopped his chair gamely enough, the neck of a brandy bottle protruding from his hip pocket. It seemed to Henry that he had had to wait an eternity for his turn, but in fact the chairs came round so rapidly that it was less than a minute after the Colonel had boarded the lift that Henry—only partly reassured by Emmy's encouraging smile—found himself waiting in the appointed spot for the next down-travelling chair to complete its circuit by clanking round the huge wheel in the shed; a couple of seconds later it came up and hit him in the back of the knees. He sat down, and the ascent began.

The ride up to the Bella Vista was certainly cold: and over some of the more precipitous ravines Henry found it advisable to keep his eyes focused stubbornly on the heights to come, rather than glancing down to the huddled, snowy rocks below.

But there was a magic, too, in the slow, steady, silent ascent—silent, that is, apart from the clatter and rattle each time the chair passed a pylon: and yet the unnerving effect of this noise was counteracted by a momentary sense of security, for the inspection platform of the pylon passed a mere eighteen inches below his dangling feet, and, noticing that a steel ladder led down from the platform to the ground below, Henry hoped fervently that if the lift did decide to break down, it would do so when he was passing a pylon, rather than at a moment when he was suspended over a precipitous gorge.

To the right, about ten feet away, was the downward cable of the lift, on which a procession of empty seats followed each other towards the valley with the stately melancholy of a deserted merry-go-round. Just occasionally, however, a down-going chair was occupied—generally by a booted and be-furred lady of uncertain years. It was very much, Henry reflected, like being on an escalator in the London underground, watching the faces that glided downwards as one ascended, to come face to face and level for a fleeting moment before the inexorable machinery churned on. When it came to scenery, however, all resemblance disappeared. Instead of the garish rectangles of advertisement which London Transport provides for the entertainment of its passengers, there were vistas of snow, cloud and mountain, of pine trees and pink rock, of misty valleys and sun-touched peaks. At last, a tiny hut came into view at the top of an open snowfield—the trees were all but left behind. As the chair approached, a little wizened man with a walnut-brown face stood ready to take Henry's arm and help him as he slid maladroitly out of the chair before it clattered on round the wheel to begin its descent.

Emmy came sailing up serenely on the next chair, slipped gracefully out of it, and came over to stand beside Henry.

"Well," she said, "here we are. And isn't it wonderful?"

Far, far below them, Santa Chiara looked like a toy village laid out on a nursery floor, the minuscule houses dotted haphazardly round the apricot-pink church. Ahead, over the ridge where the ski-lift ended, a shallow, saucer-shaped sweep of snowfields stretched away to still more mountain peaks; and to the right, round the bend of a snow-banked path, was the Albergo Bella Vista. The rest of the party were already walking up the path to the hotel, stopping every few yards to draw each other's attention to some fresh beauty. Henry and Emmy followed them slowly, hand in hand and very much at peace.

# CHAPTER THREE

ONE OF THE CHARMS of mountain architecture is its consistency. The deep eaves and steep roof-tops, the wooden balconies and shuttered windows, have been universal above a certain altitude for centuries—simply because they are functional, providing the greatest comfort and security for men living among the snows. So the Albergo Bella Vista looked exactly like any other mountain chalet, with its neat mosaic of stacked firewood nudging one wall, its balcony-veranda and pale wooden shutters pierced with heart-shaped holes.

In the hall—floors and walls of honey-coloured waxed pine—a man in a light blue suit, plump as a capon and with sparse grey hair trained carefully to hide his pink baldness, was oozing welcome.

"Allow me to present myself… Rossati, Alberto…welcome to the Bella Vista, *meine Herrschaften*…ah, welcome back Colonel Buckfast…Herr Staines…if you would kindly sign the register… this way, *bitteschoen*…may I have your passports, please…"

One by one the travellers signed in, surrendered passports, were allotted keys. By this time the luggage had arrived, having made the ascent on one of the two tray-shaped luggage carriers attached to the chair-lift. At last all was sorted out, and Henry and Emmy found themselves alone in their bedroom. It was of light wood, like the rest of the building—the floor bare of carpets, yet warm to the touch, for an enormous radiator shimmered heat from below the window. The big intricately carved bed had, in place of blankets, two vast white downy quilts, a foot thick and light as thistledown. A very large wardrobe, a plain deal dressing table, a washbasin and two upright chairs completed the furniture.

An exchange in Italian with the chambermaid elicited the information that a bath was certainly available, at the price of 500 lire.

"That's more than five shillings," said Henry, outraged.

"Baths are always a terrible price in the mountains," said Emmy, cheerfully. "I never reckon on having more than one a week. But just at the moment I think it would be cheap at a pound."

So they bathed luxuriously, and changed into clean clothes, and by a quarter to seven were ready to face the world and an apéritif.

The bar ran the whole length of the building, one side of it being composed entirely of windows, which gave onto the veranda. It was dark outside, for the moon was not yet up, but still the snow glimmered faintly white below the ink-black sky. The furniture consisted of little tables covered in red gingham tablecloths, milk-white wooden chairs, and a long chromium bar with stools upholstered in deep red leather. On the bar, inevitably, an Espresso machine hissed and wheezed like a cauldron of snakes. Henry and Emmy perched themselves on stools, and a dark, smiling girl served them with Campari-sodas. There was only one other customer in the bar—a man who sat at a table in the farthest corner and toyed with a glass of tomato juice.

Indicating the stranger with the tiniest nod of her head, Emmy whispered, "Doesn't look like a skiing type to me."

Henry half-turned to look. He saw a small, smooth man in his fifties: everything about him was chubby, from his fat little fingers caressing the stem of his glass to his short, stumpy feet, whose outline could not be disguised by his tapering suede shoes. His face was pink, round and benevolent, with small eyes that twinkled obscurely behind thick-lensed spectacles.

After a minute or so Signor Rossati, the proprietor, came into the bar. He went quickly over to the man in the corner, and spoke to him quietly in German. The man nodded amiably, finished his drink, and the two went out together, deep in conversation. They crossed the hall and Henry heard the door of Rossati's private office click shut, cutting off the voices.

"Our host seems to be bilingual," Emmy remarked.

"Nearly everyone is, in these parts," Henry replied. "We're only just over the Austrian border, you know, and this province was part of Austria until 1919. Italian is the official language now, but German comes far more naturally to a lot of the people—especially in the smaller villages."

"Does it rankle at all, I wonder—being handed over arbitrarily to Italy?" asked Emmy.

"Officially, no. Unofficially—yes, of course. But strictly under the surface. Nothing must upset the tourist trade." Henry turned to the barmaid. "Do you speak English—*parla Inglese*?" he asked.

She giggled, shook her head, and said she didn't.

"*Tedeschi*?"

Her face lit up. "*Ja, ja.*" A quick stream of German followed, but Henry just smiled and shook his head negatively.

To Emmy, he said, "You see? I'm not letting on I understand her, because I don't want our English chums to know I speak German or Italian. But you heard what she said?"

"She went too fast for me," said Emmy. "My German isn't all that good, you know. The best that can be said for it is that it's better than my Italian."

"Well," said Henry, "she was saying that German was her mother-tongue, and she'd be delighted to speak it with us since we don't know Italian. It would be quite a relief, she said."

Suddenly the hall outside became shrill with a babble of Italian voices and a cheerful stamping of boots.

"The *sci*-lift...finish..." said the barmaid.

Through the open door, Henry saw the Baroness following Gerda and the children upstairs. A man's voice said, "Maria-Pia..." and she stopped, letting the others go on ahead of her. A dark young Italian, in extremely elegant royal blue ski trousers, moved into Henry's line of vision. He stood at the foot of the staircase, and placed a hand on the Baroness's arm, restraining her, and talking urgently but softly. Gently, she freed her arm, shaking her head, but he caught her hand in his, pulling her down the stairs towards him. At that moment, Gerda reappeared round the bend of the staircase, her pale face impassive. Abruptly, the young man released the Baroness's hand, made some laughing remark, and ran upstairs past the two women, taking the steps two at a time. Gerda said something to the Baroness and they walked upstairs together. Meanwhile, Henry was amazed to see Colonel Buckfast and Roger Staines come in, dressed in full skiing regalia, their boots caked in snow.

"*Signori Inglesi*...very much *sci*...already today..." said the barmaid, trying hard. "Co-lon-el Back-fist, he *sci molto*... you not *sci*?"

"Not yet," said Henry.

"There's a nasty, icy side-slip halfway down Run Three," the Colonel was saying, in the hall. "Sensible of you to stick to Number One."

"I'm taking Run Three first thing in the morning," said Roger, defensively. "I just thought the light was a bit tricky for it this evening."

"Very wise. Never run before you can walk," said the Colonel, maddeningly. Then, in a lower tone, he added, "That cove Fritz Hauser is here again. Remember him? I saw him in Rossati's office as I went out. Don't like the fellow."

"Hauser? Oh yes, the fat little German…was here last year…can't think why he comes when he doesn't ski…"

They went upstairs.

Dinner started gaily enough. The Baroness, ravishing in black velvet trousers and a white silk shirt, sat alone—but talked merrily and loudly to the dark young Italian, who also had a table to himself. Gerda, presumably, took her dinner upstairs with the children, for there was no sign of her. The Buckfasts (Mrs. Buckfast resplendent in lilac crêpe) made quite a thing about their "usual" table, which was no different from any other, but somehow established seniority. Henry and Emmy, at Jimmy's expansive invitation, joined up with the three young English at a large table in the middle of the room. The other diners were an unmistakably German family—a comfortably plump, blonde woman in her forties, an upright, sallow-faced man with a deep scar on his cheek, and a buxom girl, presumably their daughter, who wore no makeup, had her hair twisted into unbecoming earphone plaits, and never spoke a word. At a table in the corner, Fritz Hauser ate alone, rapidly and with serious concentration.

Roger was full of his first run of the season.

"The snow's still difficult," he announced, pontifically. "Not quite enough of it, unfortunately—it was far better this time last year. Still, it's quite simple if you know how to manage it."

"I for one certainly don't," said Henry. "I intend to enrol in the ski school first thing tomorrow morning."

There was a chime of agreement from Jimmy and Caro.

"I'll come along with you," boomed Colonel Buckfast from his table, not to be outdone by Roger. "Just to introduce you, of course. I know them all down there. Splendid lot of chaps. You want to get Giulio, if you can. Best instructor in the place. Failing him, his brother Pietro. They're the sons of old Mario, you know—man who works the top end of the chair-lift. Used to be the star instructor himself until he crocked himself up."

The Colonel settled back in his chair with a comfortable affability, delighted at having established his claim to local knowledge.

Before anybody else could speak, the Baroness said quietly, "Giulio is dead."

"What!" Roger dropped his spoon into his soup plate with a clatter, swinging round to look at the Baroness. Then, conscious that his own party were staring at him, he muttered, "I mean, I knew him quite well. He taught me when I was here last year."

"I say—I'm damned sorry to hear that," said the Colonel, who had turned a deep raspberry red. He looked genuinely distressed, but whether on account of Giulio's death, or because somebody else had found out about it before he had, Henry could not be certain.

"How did it happen, eh?" the Colonel went on. "He was only a lad."

"It was a skiing accident, so they told me in the village," said the Baroness. After a pause, she added: "Last week."

"He was a young man of great…great foolishness." The dark young Italian joined in, speaking very earnestly, partly from deep sincerity and partly because he found English difficult. "This was not surprise. If not ski…then that so-rapid automobile he drive…no chains…he must die."

"He was on the Immenfeld run, just over the Austrian border," the Baroness went on. "It's very dangerous terrain there, and the run was definitely prohibited because of the snow conditions. But just because it was forbidden, Giulio must attempt it. He was like that. They found him at the bottom of a crevasse. One ski was still on his foot. The other ski and his sticks they never found."

There was an awkward pause.

"Poor old Mario," said the Colonel at last, wiping his moustache with his napkin.

There was a clatter of wood on wood as Fritz Hauser got up and replaced his chair neatly at his table. Only he and the German family seemed quite unmoved by the conversation. "They probably don't understand English," thought Emmy.

Hauser stopped at the Germans' table, said something in a low voice to the girl, and crossed the room to the door. There he paused, as if taking a decision. Then he turned and said in good English to the room in general: "This idiot Giulio is dead. So—it is his own fault. He disobeyed orders. Let it not be a discouragement to other skiers." He gave a curious little bow, and walked out.

"What a vile little man," said Caro.

"Yet it is true what he was saying," said the Baroness. "There is nothing to fear if one is sensible. Only the foolish come to grief."

"That's what I always say." Mrs. Buckfast spoke firmly and surprisingly. "You just have to be a little careful." All at once, Henry had an extraordinary impression of tension, as if each remark had more than its surface meaning, as if purposeful streams of innuendo were being directed by the speakers towards—whom? Everybody? One other person? He glanced round. Caro was looking uncomfortable, her eyes on her plate. Roger had pushed his food away, and seemed really distressed. The Colonel brooded, chin on chest. As quickly as it had come, the impression faded, became ridiculous. The Baroness remarked that it was a great tragedy, but that these things happened, and they mustn't let it spoil their holiday. She added that since the ice had now been broken, she'd like to introduce them all to Franco di Santi—the dark young Italian—who was a sculptor from Rome, whom she had met here on a previous visit. "So we are old friends," she added, with a dazzling smile.

This restored the conversation to normal, and when they had all professed themselves delighted to know Franco, Roger asked the Colonel pointedly if he intended to try the Gully—which was, as he explained to the others, the most direct but also the most precipitous route from the hotel to the village. The Colonel answered tartly that he had made enquiries about it, and that the *piste* was closed until further notice, owing to the extremely dangerous state of the run. Fearing that this might lead the conversation back to Giulio's foolhardiness, Emmy asked Roger how the residents of the Bella Vista generally spent their evenings, isolated as they were. Roger brightened up and said there was a damn good radiogram in the bar, and why didn't they all go and dance?

"What about that poor little German wretch," said Jimmy *sotto voce*, indicating the other table. "Let's ask her to join us."

"Yes, let's," said Caro, in a stage whisper. "The poor thing looks too bullied for words."

Henry hoped for politeness' sake that the German family did not understand English: certainly they gave no sign of knowing that they were being talked about, but continued to plough stolidly through monoliths of cheese and dishes of gherkins.

"You ask her, Roger old dear," said Jimmy. "You're the expert in Hun-talk."

"Yes, go on, Roger darling," said Caro.

With some reluctance, Roger got up and went over to the other table. They saw him exerting his not inconsiderable charm as he proffered the invitation: his reception, however, was quite brutally abrupt. Before the girl could say a word, her father rasped out a curt refusal, and all three got to their feet and stumped out of the dining room. Roger returned to the table looking crestfallen and angry.

"Charming, I must say," he remarked, dropping into his chair again.

"What did he say, the old pig?" asked Caro, solicitously.

"Just bellowed that it was out of the question, and dragged the poor kid off before she could open her mouth," Roger answered.

"A maiden in distress…how splendid." Jimmy was enjoying himself, and his conspiratorial glee was infectious. "We must rescue her from the dragon's clutches. Who knows where her room is?"

Caro volunteered that she had seen the girl coming out of the room opposite hers on the top floor. "And my room's at the back," she added, "so hers must be over the front door."

"All right then," said Jimmy. "We'll wait until they've all gone to bed, and then Roger and I will climb up to her balcony and serenade her—"

"Don't be silly, everyone would hear you," objected Caro.

"We'll serenade her very quietly," said Jimmy a little severely. "Then she can leave a bolster in her bed and creep downstairs…"

Still plotting delightedly, they all adjourned to the bar. "…and if that old bastard comes down and makes a scene," Jimmy was saying, "I promise you I'll—"

He stopped abruptly. From the bar came the strains of a sentimental Neapolitan love song, recorded by a lush tenor to an accompaniment of dreamy guitars: and through the open door they could see the persecuted damsel waltzing sedately with Fritz Hauser, while her parents sipped coffee and Italian brandy at a table.

Emmy burst out laughing. "So much for your maiden in distress," she said.

Poor Jimmy came in for a lot of good-natured teasing, which he took with his usual equanimity. Soon they were all dancing. The Baroness danced once with Roger and several times with Franco, and then said she was exhausted and wanted to be up early next morning to ski. Soon after she had gone, Henry and Emmy decided that they, too, were ready for bed, and Franco agreed with them. When they left, Roger and Caro were demonstrating the cha-cha-cha to Jimmy, while Colonel Buckfast ordered just one more brandy, positively the last tonight, and Mrs. Buckfast complained that the Italians would never learn to make good English coffee.

Lying in bed, Emmy reached out a hand to put out the light, and said, "Poor Jimmy. His Sir Galahad act fell a little flat."

"Yes." Henry's voice was heavy with sleep. "Still, who knows…he may need it again one of these days…"

Emmy raised herself on one elbow. "You mean she wasn't enjoying herself with Hauser?"

"Well, would you?"

"I don't know. He seems quite a reasonable little fellow. Henry—"

"Mm." Henry was almost asleep.

"Henry, do you think the Baroness came here for a secret assignation with Franco di Santi? He's terribly good-looking, and I'm certain he's in love with her…"

"Oh, go to sleep," muttered Henry into his pillow.

In the silence that followed, the sound of the gramophone drifted up faintly to them, rhythmic and cloying. Emmy's last waking thought was of the unknown young man, Giulio, lying frozen and alone at the bottom of the ravine, with one ski still strapped to his foot.